PRAISE FOR

Sensation

"Nick Mamatas continues his reign as the sharpest, funniest, most insightful and political purveyor of post-pulp pleasures going. He is the People's Commissar of Awesome."
—China Miéville, award-winning author of *Kraken* and *The City & the City*

"Nick Mamatas's brilliant comic novel, *Sensation*, reads like an incantation that both vilifies and celebrates the complex absurdity of the modern world."
—Lucius Shepard, winner of the Hugo, Nebula, and World Fantasy awards.

"The Majestic Plural, or Royal We, is well known—*Sensation* introduces the Arachnid Plural, the we of spiders, the ones that live inside you. The spiders care about you—deeply—and want to use you in a millennial war against certain parasitic wasps. No, I was wrong. The spiders only want to help. So let them in."
—Zachary Mason, *New York Times* bestselling author of *The Lost Books of the Odyssey*

★ SENSATION

★

SENSATION

Nick Mamatas
PM PRESS
2011

★

Chapter 3 previously appeared under the title "In the Glow" in *Per Contra* no. 14, Summer 2009.

ISBN: 978-1-60486-354-3
LCCN: 2010916473

PM Press
P.O. Box 23912
Oakland, CA 94623
pmpress.org

Printed in the USA on recycled paper.

Cover: John Yates/Stealworks.com
Layout: Jonathan Rowland

For Olivia, again.

Acknowledgements

They say that the more books one writes, the fewer people one needs to acknowledge. With my next novel, I might finally find myself at the stage GG Allin reached when he dedicated an album to "no-fucking-body but me." But with *Sensation*, I had help.

First I'd like to thank my sister Teddie Mamatas, who lent me her home and computer, and went on errands for everything from printer paper to brownies while I finished the last, uh, forty thousand words of this fifty-three thousand-word book. Paola Corso and Shouhua Qi, both of Western Connecticut State University, advised and supported the writing of my MFA thesis, which this book is. Brian Cully helped with the temporary disabling of the World Wide Web, and Chris Bell pitched in with the true-life story of his long working hours in otherwise "frozen" southern Manhattan in the days immediately after the terror attack of 9/11. Seth Cully didn't mind that I stole his joke about feet and alternative modes of transportation.

Of course, I should also thank my agent Michele Rubin, who gave me some excellent career advice: "Write a Don DeLillo book. You know, something with jokes, but they aren't funny." (We both agree that I failed.) Then there's credit due to transnational capitalism, the temporary collapse of which in 2008 eventually led me back to my first love—punk-influenced, politically charged, independent presses. Ramsey Kanaan paid an advance partially in the form of a PM Press-branded hoodie, and Andrea Gibbons did a whole lot of everything.

Thanks again, everyone.

1

Raymond saw his ex-wife twice—both times by accident—in the first few months after she went into hiding. The context in which Raymond first saw Julia after her murder of Peter Neads Fishman was so bizarre to him that he didn't even realize it was her at first. She was at the Food Emporium on the corner of West 12th Street and Sixth Avenue, where she never ever shopped before, and her shopping cart was stocked with items he knew she didn't eat.

She even wrote a check, pulling her checkbook from the purple purse—*Purple!* thought Raymond—and filling out every line while two of the other customers behind her silently fumed. There was a third customer too, a large man of indeterminate ethnicity in whose emptied-out brainpan we rode. We cradled a gallon of skim milk like it was an infant and waited more patiently. Raymond had thought she might have been someone from high school, or maybe even the television, until she smiled at the oblivious cashier and, in response to his clipped "Have a good day," said what Julia always used to say:

"Yahbye."

Half acknowledgment, half farewell, that's what Julia had been like. She had a way of looking at Raymond, at anyone with whom she was speaking, really, that made him (or them, or you, and once even us) feel like the most important person in the world, but only so long as you kept proving it to her every few seconds. By nodding intently when she spoke. By feeding her windups for her punchlines. Raymond might fuss over some story he'd heard on NPR about the Gaza Strip and how one-state solutions to the crisis seemed so unfeasible and she'd say, "Well, you can't expect the world to give the Palestinians their own land. Look at how they live." She'd smile a statue's smile for a second and then burst into laughter at his chagrin. Then she'd move on to some other topic, or, ultimately, some other person or way of life so profoundly challenging to the status quo that we had to step in; we had to bring her from her world into ours.

In a flash, Raymond realized something, just from the twitch and curve of the pen in Julia's hand. She'd finally stopped using his surname, Hernandez, and was back to Ott. Whatever life she was living now, he was not in it. Raymond started shopping at the Food Emporium every day. He never saw Julia there again, but did frequently run into the man of indeterminate ethnicity. Vaguely Asian, but no. Saami perhaps, Raymond almost decided. He hated his tendency to pigeonhole, despite the fact that he could muster some professional interest in the subject of ethnicity and physical anthropology. He taught at City University of New York's City College. He'd published articles about the conflation of Gitano, Roma, and Travelers in dominant cultures. He also shared a laugh with Julia whenever she used the name Hernandez, which would sometimes fluster and annoy drug store clerks and the like.

"Julia looks like an icicle," Raymond's mother once complained. "An icicle topped with crabgrass hair." Julia had even gotten a minority scholarship to return to grad school—MBA of all things—since no college would dare question whether or not she was actually Hispanic. A discreet inquiry? No. Genetic testing? Out of the question. Julia left school before graduating anyway. And yet, there Raymond was, struggling with the large man of indeterminate ethnicity.

The man's ethnicity was indeterminate by design, thanks to careful breeding, the manipulation of both genes and diet, and a large amount of tubiliform silk and choreography. We live inside his left ear, and in many other places. We kept an eye on Julia, but we also now had to keep an eye on Raymond.

He'd been at the Food Emporium that day because he'd suddenly been caught up in the memory of the texture of Entenmann's Rich Frosted Donuts. The way the chocolate coating, hard and plasticky, split on his tongue. The meat of the doughnut, thick and spongy like it was made a day old. Objectively, these were not the qualities Raymond enjoyed in doughnuts. But that day he was slain in the spirit of Entenmann's Rich Frosted Donuts, and Whole Foods doesn't carry them, so there he was at the Food Emporium.

Raymond thought he'd glimpsed Julia around town several other times before finally deciding to track her down. But he couldn't be sure it was her. There Raymond was, sitting on the other side of and across from her on a train car on the M line when he had to go to a dentist in his network because his regular dentist was on vacation.

And there Raymond was at Edson Carvalho Brazilian Jujitsu and Judo, staring out the second-story window during his free lesson, panting and drinking his own sweat, when she wandered by, a patch of crabgrass navigating the flesh of the streets below. She was headed east, deep into the Gramercy neighborhood that had previously been too boring for Julia.

Bellevue is out that way, isn't it? Raymond asked himself. Then he felt a tug on his borrowed judogi and returned to the mat to practice being strangled.

And there Raymond was, at 11:11 p.m. on a Thursday night at Times Square, after just having left a performance of a revival of *How To Succeed In Business Without Really Trying* with a woman he'd not see again after one tepid kiss and her quick *sortie* down the steps of the subway station, looking up at the huge digital displays of stock prices and headlines and the president's giant low-resolution head, noting the time and making a wish as he always did whenever he saw it was 11:11, and there was Julia next to him, chin high, doing the same, as she used to do when they were together. As she taught him to do when they had met ten years ago, on their first date. That was an 11:11 a.m. This time, this 11:11 p.m., he knew it was her.

You might think Raymond turned to say something and Julia was gone. That's how it goes. *And he turned to face her, but she was gone. Raymond stood alone under the throb and thrum of Time Square's electric cathedral.* But no, Julia was still there, and she smiled and put her eyes wide, expectantly, and I was behind them, in my large man of indeterminate ethnicity, ready to push Raymond into traffic, to end him right then and there, but his autonomic nervous system was wiser than his heart and he ran.

ONE year ago, Julia was stung by *Hymenoepimescis sp.*, a wasp native to Panama that due to lackadaisical Customs procedures had managed to find its way to Long Island, specifically to the basement of the Stony Brook home of Julia's mother-in-law in a box of old blankets that a relative had sent to the United States as a demonstration of disgust with Julia's mother-in-law, Lynn. *Here*, the box of blankets seemed to say, *you should be living like this, under these awful, stained blankets, not I!*

Further, the basement itself had high radon levels, as sometimes happens on Long Island. The risks associated with living in the home of Lynn Hernandez are the equivalent of smoking ninety-eight packs of cigarettes a day. The *Hymenoepimescis sp.* colony, nonsmokers all, had mutated significantly over the course of the seven generations they lived in the basement. Normally, such wasps don't even build nests. *We* are their nests.

In nature, *Hymenoepimescis sp.* reproduces by conspiring against the *Plesiometa argyra* spider. Against us. The wasp attacks and lays its eggs within the spider's abdomen. The larvae consume the spider's haemolymph and then excrete a chemical that changes the spider's behavior. Instead of the web *Plesiometa argyra* usually builds, the chemical compels the spider to create a box-web design that can support the weight of the pupating wasp. After the web is done, the larvae eat the spider and build a cocoon in the strong web, then pupate.

In this particular sliver of nature, the wasp attacked Julia Hernandez, *née* Ott, and laid its eggs under Julia's dermis. The larvae consumed some of Julia's blood, stuffing themselves to gorging and appearing rather like a blood blister. Julia, after several days of dizziness and a swollen forearm which looked rather frightful, even for a wasp sting, and was treated for the wound by a physician chosen by Julia's managed care provider for his ability to send patients home after a cursory examination without the slightest pang of professional guilt. He missed the eggs, of course. Julia was also given a course of levofloxacin, an antibiotic so popular amongst physicians that they call it, amongst themselves, "Vitamin L." The doctor wasn't expecting Julia to have a bacteriological infection from the sting, but he found that prescription medication helped shut patients up. Plus, they would often call when the course was over and he could then do a phone consultation. Without medication, too many patients went home and just stayed there, feeling intermittently sick from their symptoms.

In this case, however, levofloxacin gave Julia a false sense of security. She was sure that the drugs could handle any negative effects of the wasp sting, but of course antibiotics are not proof against oviposited mutant *Hymenoepimescis sp.* larvae. So when Julia began feeling peculiar urges, she didn't think to connect her innovative new ideas about life, society, and her role in it, to her day down in her mother-in-law's basement, where she was looking for Raymond's old comic books so that she could sell them on eBay and go to Greece for the summer.

Two months later, Julia, who was working at a Web 3.0 design firm as an executive assistant, read up on programming. She created a little subroutine, one that sliced a few cents off various e-commerce transactions for firms that contracted with her employer. She didn't steal the money; indeed, she barely kept it. The few cents were held for a day, and put onto the currency markets, and the interest was deposited automatically in an unnamed account in a Cayman Islands bank. This money was not for her. Indeed, it was supposed to be for you. Millions of transactions, billions of dollars, a few cents here and there with twenty-four hours worth of interest. She was a millionaire on paper by the end of the week.

Eleven months ago, Julia decided that she would never ever cross the street with the lights again. She jaywalked constantly, as if the little white man meant stop and the big red hand meant go. She would do this late at night, when there were no cars. She did it while striding across Broadway at the end of banking hours, ignoring the shrieks of the police, the belligerent howls of cabbies, and the calls of "Hey, you dumb bitch! What the fuck!"

When stopped by the police, she'd accept the ticket, go home, and pay it online with her stolen money. Julia jaywalked a lot. She jogged through red lights. Traffic snarls in the Bronx, where the I-95 funnels cars into the city ever-so-slowly in the nigh nonexistent best of circumstances, could be traced back to Julia walking across St. Mark's Place against traffic, oblivious to everything except for the fried peanut butter and jelly sandwich she bought from the bright pink automat with the first Richard Nixon dollar coins to be issued. Gas prices rose by 1.9 cents on the island of Manhattan due to increased usage by idling traffic.

Then she left Raymond. "Get up," she said, terse and tapping his shoulder. They were in the midst of an act of physical love. "Get off." It was 12:34 a.m and Raymond had penetrated her six minutes prior.

"Are you okay?" he asked.

"Oh yes," she said, instantly reassuring, her voice half a coo. Then she twisted her lips, as if hiding something. Raymond shifted to the right, bumping her thigh with the back of his hips and let her go. She slipped on a pair of panties and then her T-shirt. She reached back over the bed and retrieved her blue jeans, which had been crumpled up and under one of their pillows.

"Where are you going? What's the matter?" Raymond said. No coo would sooth him then.

"Oh, I'm leaving you," Julia said. She had her duffle bag out and was randomly scooping up clothing from her two drawers in their shared dresser.

"What?"

Julia looked at Raymond closely. "I'm not going to give you a reason. I like you like this. I like the idea that your stomach just turned to concrete. That you might be ready to threaten me, maybe even hit me." Raymond's fists were balled up, as they often were when he was frustrated, but he hadn't even thought of punching Julia, of grabbing a fistful of her hair and swinging her head against the side of the doorjamb, until she'd said that.

"Don't say a fucking word. I have to see how long it will take for me to have another cock inside me. I'm aiming for under an hour." She reached into her duffle and produced a derringer. It looked chrome-kitschy, like some obscure instrument for applying eye make-up, or like something one might buy at Restoration Hardware to express a desire to be thought of as a person who liked to drink gin and read Hemingway, and she pointed it lazily at Raymond. He thought about trying to snatch it. Derringers fired small bullets, .22s. He knew that from somewhere. It's hard to kill someone with a .22, unless you shoot them in the eye. That last part he guessed. While Raymond considered leaping onto the gun, Julia kicked her feet into her pumps and stepped backwards out the door of their bedroom, then the kitchen, and left. He heard her walking down the hallway past the thin walls of the apartment, her duffle scraping along the banister.

Raymond decided definitely not to call his mother, though he really wanted to. He could still feel her on the hair of his crotch.

Three weeks after Julia left Raymond, she became incredibly famous.

Wars, *contra* the old saying, do not rage. Wars simmer. Small squads happen upon one another and open fire. Jets scream through the skies, launching missiles and dropping bombs, but for most on the ground, in deep tunnels or basements or caves, these sorties are just moments of thunder followed by years of slow and smoldering ruin. Then there are the insurgents, planning their little plans ever so slowly, trading chickens and old silverware for copper wire and car batteries that work, just for a single "improvised" explosive device. Everyone is involved in an insurgency, it's a war of all against some, but only tangentially. One woman has some powder, a man a clock that that he found in the trashed remains of an apartment building. Another fellow has a will to kill that outstrips his will to live. They work together, through a network of cousins and co-religionists and school chums who remember the good old days when bread was cheap enough to occasionally just let spoil on a countertop. That's war simmering to a slow boil it can never reach. War is hell, but only if hell is other people and other people are generally speaking both quite boring and extremely—if not necessarily rationally—self-interested.

War, in its simmering, is not a good match for the twenty-four hour news cycle. Reporters do not knock on doors, asking for the skinny on the old lead pipes that used to be rusting in some backyard but that quickly disappeared. None will ask an American GI how many times per week he masturbates, and whether the sand scratches his glans. The end result is that trauma of the vacuum of war, the void in which there are an insufficient number of sympathetic corpses to fill the white gap on the front pages and the grey hum of the screens: the slow news day.

And on a slow news day, Julia made her first public move. She had spent three days in Brooklyn, in a neighborhood with no crisp grid of streets and avenues. There was a different sense of things here, by the Atlantic Yards. History, layered like a sandwich or piles of leaves in a small old wood. Italians aging and dying, living in the homes built by stout WASPs and Germans, funded by the rails stretching past the horizon and to golden California, and beneath that flat farmland and streets stamped solid by foot and hoof. You needed to know your seventeenth-century Dutch history to really intuit your way around Brooklyn, and the stories of the second-rate robber barons that fell off the great island of Manhattan and ended up on the tip of the long island to recoup and build their own mausoleums to the self. Julia had said to herself, "Let's get lost," and she, and those *Hymenoepimescis sp.* itching under her skin, surely did get lost to all but us, and our men of indeterminate ethnicity.

Julia was white, and had a purse full of money, and wasn't shy. She spent a lot of time in diners, staying far too long into the night, recharging with coffee and pancakes, and reading the free weekly newspapers and pick-up magazines that littered the streets till the seats went up onto the tables, thanks to our arms and backs. Were Julia a character in a movie, perhaps a waiter would have taken her home, or maybe she would be given an apron and a job right on the spot by the burly Greek owner, because she looked so sad yet strong. But Julia was not a character in a movie, and could hardly be said to look sad at all. Her eyes were wild like the streets used to be, before the neighborhood was gutted for the stadium and the high rises.

Julia showered at the Y and bought new clothes at local stores—"what am I bid?" fishnets, and pencil skirts, and T-shirts with rhinestones and winking cats on them.

And tiny boots. She made friends on her second night, thanks to a broad red smear of lipstick and the quivering excitement of thirty hours awake. It was at the Kellogg's Diner, whose old sign hinted at some ancient relationship with the cereal company, in a ratty booth. A young man and woman, skinny in striped shirts, with Buddy Holly glasses (matching) and haircuts (similar, but not identical) that Julia decided to christen The Institutional as it seemed like the kind of work a state employee with a head shaver and a spastic client might do as part of mental hospital intake. They had a petition, Julia had a smile.

"We oppose the construction of the stadium and the new condos," the woman explained. Her name was Alysse, she said, and she was worried about rising rents, increased traffic loads, and the decline of working-class neighborhoods and ethnic diversity. The man, her boyfriend surely given the body language and peculiar choose-shirts-from-the-same-pile-on-the-floor wardrobe they were both a-rockin', nodded in agreement. He was called Davan. Julia told them her name was Julia.

"Are you two lifelong Brooklynites?" Julia asked. "Any kids?"

"No, but I've been here a long time," Davan said. "Three years."

"Eight months for me," Alysse said. Julia nodded in a way that compelled a couple to slide into the seat on the other side of her booth.

"Gentrification, eh?" Julia said. Davan spread out flyers, a clipboard, pictures of the proposed stadium and a poor black child holding a toy, and a leaflet with a grotesque caricature of Peter Neads Fishman, his head like a swollen light bulb and nose a frankfurter.

"This neighborhood used to have character," Davan said, "It still does, really," said Alysse, with a wave around the diner.

"Isn't the stadium already a *fait accompli*?" Julia asked. And indeed, the stadium, at least partially constructed and wrapped in a web of scaffolding and flapping tarpaulin, was clearly visible through the window of the booth in which the three were sitting.

"It's about consciousness," Davan said. "Remembering history."

"Yeah. That's what it is for me. I mean, I didn't even know there was a problem after I moved here, and then I met Davan. Why can't I live in a neighborhood that isn't been torn up to make way for some decamillionaires to buy condos from a billionaire?" Alysse said. Julia just stared, a forkful of pancake dripping syrup back onto the plate by her mouth. The fork was smeared with red from her lipstick. Then Alysse added, "Well, why can't I live in *this* neighborhood without a stadium and the condos?"

"Because the stadium and the condos are already there."

Davan smiled. "Yeah, well, it's not like we can blow it up. But we can limit its impact. Payouts to displaced families. The minimum plan for new construction around the stadium. Light rail."

"I don't agree with the light rail," Alysse said. "I'm a traditionalist. I like the grand old subway stations, even if the paint is flaking off the pillars and the tiles are cracked and the public restrooms are closed forever."

"They stink like pee, the subway stops around here," Julia said. "I suppose because the restrooms are closed forever. One of those unintended consequences, I suppose."

Neither Davan nor Alysse quite knew what to say in response, so they laughed, Davan more than Alysse. He liked the idea of an attractive woman speaking about urination while eating pancakes in a greasy spoon. "It felt like a sliver of authenticity in a world of contrivance," he would later write in a blog read by a handful of his friends, and by Raymond as well.

Julia took the clipboard and signed her name to the petition, then crossed out her maiden surname and wrote Raymond's name, Hernandez, next to it. She wrote the address of the Kellogg Diner itself as her address, and a phony but plausible-seeming email address for her contact information. "Now what?" she asked, sliding the clipboard back.

"Thanks," Alysse said, and she moved as if she wanted to slide out of the booth, but Davan was rooted in his seat. "Well, we're raising consciousness here," he said. "We have extra petitions, if you want to start collecting signatures. It's not that we're going to submit the signatures to Fishman—you can't change a man's mind against his own interests, at least not when they're as rich as Fishman, and have the city council as personal servants—but it's a way to start conversations."

"We're autonomists," Alysse said, believing that the word explained it all. Julia made a gesture somewhere between a shrug and the anxious wave of one's hands you might see an impatient shopper do at the supermarket when two carts want the same patch of space in an aisle.

"We don't believe in telling people what to do," Alysse said. "I mean, who are we to come into this neighborhood and tell the families here to go out and protest, or to try to lead them?"

"That would make us as bad as Fishman," Davan said.

Julia nodded, her chin wrinkled in a mimicry of thoughtfulness. "Yes," she said.

"I mean, it would be great if people around here would just wake up," Davan said. "And do something. Picket, stop the construction workers from coming onto the site. The project only needs to fall behind a few months for the entire sports season—basketball, hockey, the circus, all sorts of things—to be fouled up. He'll lose millions, maybe even fail to complete it."

"It could become a community garden, or a homeless shelter, or something for the people," Alysse said.

"It could at least stop subsequent investment that doesn't take into account the community." Davan said.

Julia nodded. "But you don't want to tell anyone to do this, or arrange it with anyone?"

Davan leaned back in the booth, the cheap uphol-stery squeaking under him, and held open his arms. "We're not Malcolm X here. We can only make sugges-tions. And ask people to take their own petitions and spread the meme."

Julia said, "Meme?"

"An idea, in people's heads. They're like genes, they propagate themselves. A 'do something' meme. If we talk to one hundred people, and ten of them take the meme and it evolves into ten new ideas—"

"Descendents of the original, primordial idea," Alysse said, interrupting.

"And that means ten modes of attack on the devel-opment process, ten modes which likely cannot be pre-dicted—" Davan continued.

"Or stopped." The couple smiled together, like they practiced it often, or lived in an apartment so small that their habits and expressions could not help but be mixed together, like their CD collections.

"Well, what are you going to do about memes like 'I can walk to a Nets game and not have to pay for parking,' or 'Working-class families are boorish and gauche and some expensive condos will bring in a bunch of nice white kids with money to spend on pancakes and photocopies'?" Julia asked. She winked too, and the tip of her tongue darted out to catch a drop of syrup on her lip.

"Yeah, or 'Who are these two particular white kids who haven't even lived here very long pretending to be outraged by gentrification?' right?" asked Alysse in return.

Julia said "Just so," and Davan huffed, sitting up very straight. Julia leaned in close and said, conspiratorially, "Have we just infected you with our memes, David?"

"Davan," said Davan. Julia glanced over at Alysse, who appeared bemused.

"Davan," Julia said, "I'll be right back." And she got up and left the diner. Alysse noticed for the first time that Julia didn't have a purse or even a coat, and the night was fairly chilly. "Bye!" Alysse called out, ready to say something else, to intervene somehow, but Julia only said, "Yahbye!" and trotted through the exit.

After three minutes, when the check came and Julia had not yet returned, Davan figured something out as well. Alysse paid the bill, because it wasn't fair to the waitress if the diner was stiffed, and because Davan's freelance job as a graphic designer is generally either feast or famine, and this month was all famine.

☆ ☆ ☆

JULIA went to the Y, where her stash of cash was kept in a locker, and removed seventy-five dollars. From there she stopped at several bodegas and dollar stores, buying cheap white soap—Ivory mostly, but various off-brand soaps as well, some with names and lists of ingredients presented in Spanish. At one, she even bought a two-wheeled wagon in which to carry the soap.

By 1 a.m., Julia had reached the stadium. Scaffolding is hard to climb, she found out quickly enough. Julia could never do a pull-up. But, in the maze of barriers that sealed off the sidewalk on both sides, Julia found an opening and in that opening stood a Dumpster, its flaps closed. Julia emptied her two-wheeled wagon of the bags of soap bars and placed them atop the Dumpster, then scrambled onto it herself. From there, she was able to reach the first of several catwalks with relative ease. First she hefted the bags of soap up, as she had done on the Dumpster, and followed them to the next level.

On the catwalk, Julia teetered, unsure of the planks under her feet and the sight of lampposts at eye level. The cars already began to look smaller, like toys. But still she climbed, tossing the soap up first, nine bags of stuff swung high and then pushed, and then with a sharp intake of breath she reached up and pulled herself up still higher, past the first layer of tarp and to the second.

High enough, she thought, she hoped. It was windy and cold, probably, and Julia was never a broad woman. The weather cut through her bones, even as her heart and lungs boiled in her chest from the exertions of the night, the excitement of the moment. She opened the first bag and unwrapped four bars of soap. She put the wrappers back in the plastic bag and, grabbing two bars in each hand, reached out and scraped the soap against the exterior wall of the stadium, right on the curve facing the intersection.

It took a long time and the whole of the bars to form the first letter. Julia's arms tired quickly, but she persevered. There was plenty of time till the sunrise, and she could work even through the dawn thanks to the curtain of tarps hanging behind her. After carving out the I and the J and the U, she had the thought, it seemed, that construction may begin before dawn. Isn't that everyone's complaint, after all, that jackhammers growl to life and pound the sidewalks at 7 a.m., and that morning commutes are forever being snarled by backhoes and trucks full of sewer pipe? She redoubled her efforts as best she could, sweating and dirty through the sooty night, except for her hands and arms, which were covered in the slippery scents and bubbles of soap and sweat.

Julia dreaded the possibility of making a typo—maybe she thought the word *Soap-o* because that is the sort of person she was—and wiped her eyes with the back of her arm, but only succeeded in making them sting. Soap. Her blouse, drenched, was no better. Then she tried a tarp, and the rough weave of fiberglass scratched her face, but did finally clear her eyes. She stepped back carefully, but still felt her stomach swirl up her spine like a snake on a branch. The world turned upside-down for a moment, and Julia reached out wildly for a handhold. Julia's hands were slippery and her knees buckled from the realization, and the phantom taste of a face full of concrete, but she managed to hug the lattice of metal piping, hooking the bars on the curves of her elbows. She felt a sting on her tongue, bile and vomit from the fear. It fell viscously from her mouth.

Finally, Julia turned back to her work, more careful than before, her arms taffy from the scraping of the soap to form those thick, wide letters. Every soap wrapper, each little cardboard box, was placed back into one of the plastic bags from the convenience stores. Y was triumphant, a cheerleader with arms splayed, holding pom-poms. The Us were easy, almost soothing, though they required extensive kneeling. Sadly, Julia had to make the O as a U with a little half-oval on top. The round joviality of O was beyond the medium of concrete and soap, at least given the work that had come before.

When Julia was done with the message, she turned and tried to pull the tarps from the scaffolding, but her hands were still slippery and her fingers weak and stiff from all the grasping. She tugged hard and nearly stomped her foot. Julia had to swallow that urge, just to avoid falling from the scaffold and hitting the two paths on the way down to the sidewalk. Still determined, she lowered herself down, one level at a time, like an infant scooting down a flight of steps on legs and butt, till she hit the Dumpster with a satisfying thud. She opened the flap that she wasn't standing atop, and instantly found a shark-finned shard of cement. After a quick rinse of her hands in puddle water, and drying them against her blouse, it was back up the scaffolding, and the slicing went easy.

Julia collected the bags, put the cement shard in one, and looping her arms through the handles, gingerly made her way down to the ground level, awkward as if trying to play violin with a pair of bat wings for arms. The sun was muscling its way up the river by the time she was done. Julia hopped on a bus, she didn't know which one, bags and all, and didn't get off till she was back in Manhattan.

That morning the side of the stadium, which didn't have a name yet as the rights hadn't been sold, though both Costco and the Harriman family were said to be interested, had a message for Brooklyn.

I JUST WANT YOUR HALF

Police were called, and two patrolmen dutifully appeared to write things down on their little pads. Neither knew what song it was from, though one of the construction workers, an apprentice carpenter had it stuck in his head because he drove past the old World Fair's ground in Queens that past weekend. The foreman called for the sandblaster and by 10 a.m. the morning crew had managed to permanently engrave the message into the wall. It had only been soap, after all. It rained that afternoon.

4

OVERHEARD in New York – Two Construction Guys, with hardhats and thick arms, the whole bit, standing across the street from that stupid stadium (aka the Fishbowl):

Construction Guy #1:	"I just want your half."
Construction Guy #2:	(bagel in hands) "No way."
Construction Guy #1:	(pointing to the Fishbowl) "No, yeah, really."
Construction Guy #2:	"Well you ain't getting any. Both halves are mine!"

PHOTOS of the words from that old song were captured by cell phone camera and propagated to the blogosphere just moments after the sun rose the next morning. Conspiracy, apropos, a sell-out, a prank or *détournement*. In the neighborhood, or at least in the connect-the-dots psychography of the used bookstore, the bar that opens at noon and serves savory crepes along with Pabst Blue Ribbon, the third-generation dot com firm full of sniveling technical writers who spend their days writing instructions for wireless applications that will never exist, the newsstand where one can buy the French *Vogue* three days after it hits the streets of Paris, the diner with the blueberry pecan pancakes, the L train and the F train that pull out of their stations in plus-or-minus five minutes of 8:34 and 8:22 respectively thus allowing for a quick hustle in clicking heels across a marbled lobby at 9:02 and an at-desk bagel and Orangina at 9:07 so long as the boss isn't late too and waiting by the elevator banks with a sour look on her stretched face, I JUST WANT YOUR HALF was big news.

Amongst the newspaper readers and the pre-work dog-walkers and the breakfast burrito eaters and screeching school children and those worried about the school system and property tax evaluations and the $120 barrel of oil, Julia's vandalism may as well not have occurred.

Williamsburgist.com put up the best photo of I JUST WANT YOUR HALF, and in the comments section to that morning's blog entry, an idea was offered up by a user posting under the name Snarly Temple:

> *"I Just Want Your Half"? Sounds like the slogan Fishman lives by already. Well, it works for him anyway. (I wonder if the band will sue and try to reclaim their half.) Why not for the rest of us? Let's get on the chans and start arranging something.*

Snarly Temple's comment was later credited with beginning the movement with no name, but it must be said that, like jokes, social movements often emerge in many places at once. Williamsburgist.com, the blog, was run by one Brian Bernstein, who, as a child, witnessed the space shuttle *Challenger* blowing up on television. He had the day off from school for some reason—he never could recall why—and an episode of *All In The Family* on syndication was interrupted by a news bulletin detailing the explosion. Bernstein, a nerd since 1977 when *Star Wars* came out, spent the day in a funk, yet riveted to the news. The next morning, in eighth grade homeroom—he was bussed to Coney Island each morning, to a magnet school then called Mark Twain Junior High—he was looking at the newspaper his homeroom teacher had laid across the desk, and through some spasm of perversion, was the first person in the world to coin this joke:

Q: What were the last words spoken aboard the space shuttle *Challenger*?
A: What's this button do?

★ ★ ★

Across the world, there were many other such spontaneous manifestations of gallows humor, but Bernstein's was the first.

And so too, the movement that followed in the wake of Julia's graffiti emerged from many precincts and quarters, cutting across land and time zone, but oriented toward that peculiar intersection of Generations X, Y, and Z. Largely white, surprisingly impoverished in their own eyes, people from whom the irony has never escaped, but who themselves cannot escape irony. The sort of people who might read a novel by Don DeLillo and decide that the term "child of Godard and Coca-Cola" applies to them, despite the fact that such clever-sounding untruths apply to nobody. Julia was already becoming incorrectly famous, though she never took credit for the graffiti.

Here is how the movement started. Five friends living in Brooklyn, put a video on the Internet. It was mostly text: white on a black background.

> **HELLO**
>
> WE THINK PETER NEADS FISHMAN, REAL ESTATE DEVELOPER, IS THE DEVIL
>
> WE ARE GOING TO EXORCISE HIM BUT WE NEED YOUR HELP
>
> WE JUST WANT YOUR HALF

Then a woman appeared. Alysse, actually, outside near the stadium—with the letters A, L, and F prominent behind her—spoke. "Half the money in your pockets right now. Half the rides on your MetroCard."

Cut to Davan, sitting in a small apartment's small kitchen, an elbow on a Formica-topped table. "Half the time you were going to spend masturbating this week. Half the drama you generate just by existing." Then he mugged for the camera and whimpered in a falsetto, "So lonely."

Brian Bernstein, with a neat haircut and thick shoulders. A football player gone to seed, except he never could catch a ball. "Half the time you spend being queer and here. I've already committed half the time I've previously spent getting used to it."

Another woman. Jorie Torres. Earrings like satellite dishes. "Half the time you spend compiling annoying pop culture references." She raised a fist and shook it lightly. "Autobots, roll out!"

A man in a mask. It smiles, features pointed brows and a sharp beard. Depicting Guy Fawkes, the mask was featured in a film popular a few years ago. "Half the efforts you put into making life better for yourself while increasing entropy and in some small way sending us all hurtling that much faster toward the heat death of the universe." His voice was distant-sounded and muffled by the stiff plastic of the mask, and the tiny slit that made do as a mouth hole.

Then back to black, and title cards:

> WE'RE NOT TELLING YOU WHAT TO DO
> **WE'RE JUST TELLING YOU TO DO SOMETHING**

Julia, living as she was out of a new construction condo unit in a building that had just opened to buyers, was unaware of the video. The condo had electricity but no appliances save a stainless steel refrigerator/freezer that made four kinds of ice and warned its owner when the milk was about to go bad. As remarkable as the device was, it did not have Internet access. Julia's cellular phone did have Internet access, but she didn't think to use it to check for videos featuring her slogan or Fishman. She spent the days laying on the carpeted floor, sure that passers-by would see her in the window if she walked across the empty rooms, and just as sure that she'd feel the vibrations of the hustle and blather of a thick-accented realtor coming up the steps. The wasp larvae in her blood and muscles twitched and burned, demanding action.

Graffiti covered the brick walls of the neighborhood, stencils the sidewalks. Except for the chains and franchises—McDonald's, Blimpie, Starbucks—those with the resources to pay for constant repainting of walls (no one dared sandblast anymore) Police lexica of graffiti tags and gang symbols needed daily updating. *What the fuck*, it was being asked frequently, did **I CAN HAZ NAYBURHOOD** and **GENTRIFICATION CAT IS GENTRIFIED** mean?

And not even its author knew what to make of **INVISIBLE HEGEMONIC POSTMODERN URBANIST GEOGRAPHIES**, which was sprayed across the anchorage of the Williamsburg Bridge in a glow-in-the-dark color not easily identifiable.

There were the performances—fifty people standing still as statues in the sidewalks and in the streets during morning rush, stealing moments of attention, grinding the flow of traffic to a halt. "The fishbowl makes me sick!" screamed a fifteen-year-old boy before he forced himself to vomit on Fishman at the Aleph Zadik Aleph dinner. Eight of his confederates, strategically positioned in tables all over the Great Neck catering hall joined the puke-in at that moment, splattering their suits with partially digested potatoes dyed red, white, and blue.

The Daily News ran an article covering a press conference held by Fishman spokesperson Jacques Vamos. Vamos declared that Fishman, "feeling the pain" of the neighborhood he was "attempting to improve" had come up with a "win-win solution": Fishman, Vamos said, was prepared to offer the cash equivalent to forty acres and a mule (adjusted for inflation since 1865) to any African-American family in the shadow of the Fishbowl who'd be willing to appear on television with Fishman and teach him how to dance. Fishman's actual press people quickly issued a notice pointing out that there was no Jacques Vamos in their employ.

Four hundred thousand dollars in obviously counterfeit currency—Benjamin Franklin was winking—was circulated to non-union construction employees in white envelopes marked "hush money" in lieu of their weekly paychecks. Police were able to reclaim only seventy-five thousand dollars.

Two adult women and their three children were found by security guards in the unfinished concession arcade two weeks after they set up house in the area. They had deep-fried all their meals and watched the children's Disney DVDs on the ninety-foot-tall Jumbotron after hours.

A Fishman impersonator jumped the guardrail at a live broadcast of World Wrestling Entertainment's *Monday Night Raw* and entered the ring, disrupting a match between underweight "heel" wrestler Jimmy Martini and his opponents, two little people in masks known as The Mexican Jumping Beans. Despite quick work from the technical director to pull the cameras off the Fishman impersonator, several million people still managed to identify him as Fishman as he was tackled by Martini and the referee.

Fishman's daughter, Judith, in her first year at Bennington, had sex with nine men over the course of seven days, and uploaded webcam footage of the sexual acts to the Internet.

Craig Bostwick, a realtor working for a firm that had an exclusive on several of the buildings Fishman had built in Chelsea in the middle of the decade, produced five leases allowing renters to inhabit the apartments for the sum of twenty-four dollars a month, to be paid in the equivalent amount of beads and thin plates of copper. Bostwick was fired and arrested, but was "misplaced" while being processed at One Police Plaza at the bottom of the city. He was last seen, via photos uploaded to his Myspace.com page, sitting atop a donkey in Marrakech. Tenant court found the leases to be binding, but not renewable.

In a conference room on Central Park South, immediately before a "war room" session of publicists, social psychologists, marketing personnel, and several attorneys brought together to deal with Fishman's current public relations issues, it was discovered that one bite had been taken out of every doughnut, danish, scone, bagel, bialy, sliced piece of crumb cake, and bear claw that had been set out as the morning spread for the all-day meeting.

Defrocked priest and liberation theologist Manuel Little, with the help of his three wives with whom he lived in a "Solomonic marriage," exorcized Peter Neads Fishman in a Central Park ceremony that was not attended by Fishman, but was attended by two out of three local members of the Blue Man Group.

Traditional pickets were a daily occurrence on the edges of the Fishbowl, as the stadium was quickly christened. Eager socialists in denim jackets and all-weather scarves practiced their refrain: "Want to check out a copy of *Socialist Worker*?" while smelly men and women, all bones and knotted hair, beat white plastic bucket drums and prayed for an earthquake. They were opposed, in the spirit of cooperation, by the sharp assistants of local city councilman Duane Goodwin, who was very much against the Fishbowl now that the handwriting was on the wall. Early experiences—the latter were class presidents in fifth grade or the children of not-very-indulgent lawyer parents, the former perhaps even wealthier or at least raised in the embrace of a more hysterical church—separated the groups, but little else.

Friday was, through a variety of simultaneous and independent decisions, the date of the big rally. The first public call was made by Leslie Marcovaldo—Columbia University sophomore and Goodwin intern—in conjunction with "Blue," the mysterious (to Leslie) man-child of indeterminate ethnicity, a self-identified "so-called anarchist." It was very easy to set up a decisive rally for the movement.

We simply made it clear to some of Fishman's handlers that Fishman himself should hold a press conference within the Fishbowl that afternoon. The protestors would be blocked from engaging with Fishman directly thanks to a massive deployment of NYPD personnel, as well as Fishman's private security. A "free speech zone" two blocks away would be arranged for the penning of the movement. Then, after the useless protest, Marcovaldo and others within our sphere of influence would do their work at the post-protest parties, drinking circles, and planning meetings.

This is how we tame political movements:

We find the activist fringe of the status quo, those who will pour their energy and time into an endeavor, taking personal and organizational responsibility. They have resources, expertise, rhetoric that sounds very compelling. They are success. They speak of meetings in Washington, Albany, Athens, or The Hague. How poor their grandparents, glovemakers and steam laundry workers to a person, were back when the world was scratchy and sepia-toned.

We find the aspirational fringe of the subaltern. The mighty fish of the tiniest puddles. The disaffected golden child, the wired-yet-rumpled intellectual working far beneath his or her potential. Those who will show up at every meeting, take most of the reasonable risks, who will accept payment in newspaper photos and lazy smiles from younger lovers. The men and women who buy books they'll never have the time to read; who eat fried rice they make themselves because they like it.

When we cannot find them, we make them. Then it's fairly easy. The members of the status quo with all the resources and social legitimacy make a great rush toward the target—a war, a change in legislation, the change in status of some minority or counter-hegemonic group—and then pull back. Do something else. Vote for a political party. Hold a vigil, candles lighting the night. Select a few capable individuals—the majority always from the status quo faction—and have them form a committee to negotiate a surrender. Remind the world that the movement exists by pointing out the members of the extreme faction and how threatening they are. Remind the movement that the world exists, and that it is full of semi-somnambulant television-watchers who hate all people of color and homosexuals in the name of Jesus. It works nearly always every time.

But this movement, the movement *Sans Nom* as it was called by Alysse, who always wanted to find a use for her French, was somewhat different. There would be no coalitions, no committees, no media except for the hydra-headed-and-toed Internet, and the movement hardly seemed to care at all whether any of the various actions were effective. But there was going to be Friday. Brilliant, glorious Friday, when all the movement would come together outside the Fishbowl and be reminded of their ultimate insignificance.

5

FROM http://www.williamsburgist.com/20__/07/15/trying_not_to_say_it_was_just_like_a_movie.htm

Oh God! I saw that woman kill Fishman. He was there at the podium with some lawyers and his whore wife and the construction guys and then this girl just walked up onto the stage with her little purse and smiled, like a bird or something landing on a statue's head. It was all heads and bald spots and blue safety helmets, then her wild hair and long swirly skirt.

She was pretty, or at least not a heifer, and didn't seem crazy except that she had made her way up to the stage—I snuck into the event proper and I only made it within fifty yards of the lip of the stage, by crawling up on the scaffolding. Then she reached into her purse and pulled out a silvery gun and Fishman's head exploded. I mean, the top of his head just flipped up and blood flew out like bottle rockets. And she waved the gun around back and the cops started shouting at her but the stage was so crowded with lawyers and stage-diving construction guys with feet and elbows everywhere. Then the lady just danced off, her arms flailing and the gun shining in the light.

And I mean literally, she was dancing off the stage, like she was in a musical getting her star turn finally, and all I was doing was standing there holding a stupid banner on my lap that I'd been planning on dropping and that girl just showed up and solved everything.

FISHMAN SHOOTER IDENTIFIED BY EX-HUSBAND
By Erin Carson—7/17/20__

New York, NY (AP)—The shooter of controversial real estate mogul Peter Neads Fishman has been identified as Julia Hernandez, a woman who disappeared several weeks ago from the Greenwich Village apartment she shared with her husband.

"We have a positive ID thanks to her husband, Raymond," NYPD spokesman Seth Cully said. "He called in once the footage hit the net, and we are going to find her now."

Raymond Hernandez, an assistant professor of anthropology at the City University of New York, was distraught after his wife suddenly left the home. "We weren't fighting," he told police. "She just left, telling me that she was leaving me. I'd figured it was someone else. She'd been erratic, always out of the house on some errand." Hernandez also claims that his wife brandished a gun at him but that "I'd done nothing to provoke her." Several telephone calls to Hernandez's office and home numbers have gone unanswered.

The police do not yet have a motive. "Could be the Fishbowl, but all the protests against it so far haven't added up to terrorism," said Cully. "It was a total surprise. We had the usual crowd control out there, but we have no idea how she got on stage or where she had been hiding before the event."

Fishman, 52, was a major real estate developer in Brooklyn and Manhattan for twenty years. Beginning with the rehabilitation of several storefronts on Rivington Street in Manhattan's Lower East Side, Fishman had parlayed his success and knowledge of the city's depressed neighborhoods into a personal fortune of over $100,000,000. The "Fishbowl," a 10,000-seat sports stadium critics claimed threatened the Williamsburg neighborhood in which it was being constructed, has recently been the target of several unusual protests born of an Internet-based movement with no visible leadership.

Julia Hernandez, 35, born Julia Ott in the suburbs of Cincinnati, graduated with a BA in sociology from Tufts in Boston, and worked as an insurance adjuster in western Connecticut before meeting Hernandez while pursuing a master's degree at the New School in Manhattan. She was unemployed at the time of her disappearance, but had most recently worked for Razorfish, an online firm, as an executive assistant.

UPDATED 4:34PM: Police spokesman Cully has released an updated statement reading "Could be the Fishbowl, but all the protests against it so far haven't added up to violence." The word "terrorism" should be stricken from subsequent reports.

http://www.facebook.com/note.php?note_id=47654425473898
Note: The Events of The Other Day
7/20/20__

We're all pretty messed up here, since we had met Julia a few weeks ago while canvassing and as far as Davan and I can tell, she had no idea about the stadium or Fishman until we found her and talked to her. She seemed new to Brooklyn, but nice enough. I would have guessed she was an artist.

Annoying; Davan and I had a long, screaming fight about the whole thing, and whether or not we should go to the police with what we knew about her, and about Sans Nom and all that. It doesn't even matter who started it or who had which position; I think we actually changed our minds in the middle of the fight.

Anyway, we ended up going to the police and it was a total waste of time. Davan called the local precinct and they told us to call Manhattan because the city is handling the case from there for some reason, and we called One Police Plaza. They told us to come down. I wanted to bring an attorney with us, but when we called the Center for Constitutional Rights they said they couldn't spare anybody. We went all the way down to One Police Plaza anyway, waited for three hours in a waiting room and then for twenty minutes in some detective's office, then we were told to go home. Some guy in uniform popped his head in and said, "We have nothing for you, sorry," and that was that.

From: hernanr@ccny.cuny.edu
To: [Recipient List]
Subject: Class Cancellation

To ANT 205, 225, 407. Dana W., LabenC@ccny.cuny.edu

All,

Due to extreme circumstances, with which we are
all familiar I am going to cancel all my classes and office hours for the next two weeks. Dana
and Carise, the ever-capable TAs of the 205,
will continue to run labs and are available
for help. Papers can be turned into the dropbox
outside my office.

Sorry for all who are inconvenienced by this,
but as my wife is missing and wanted for murder,
well, let us just say that circumstances beyond
my control are at work here. Visits from the police alone have been very disruptive for both my
teaching and my research.

yrs.

Dr. Hernandez, Anthropology

A LETTER RECEIVED BY JARED LAMBERSON OF WESTMONT, ILLINOIS. PURPORTEDLY FROM JULIA OTT HERNANDEZ:

Mr. Lamberson (If that is your real
name, and please imagine me saying it
slowly, as if it made me slightly ill, or
like I was that guy from *The Matrix*: Miii-
ISter Laaaaaamber-SON)

Hello! I hope this letter finds you in
good health. Are you into current events? I
hope you are, as I am a current event. Julia
Hernandez, horrid murderess and merry prank-
ster. Just dropping you this note to see
what you might do.

I am a wanted criminal, after all,

and while writing this letter on plain
white paper I found in a public library
(your address from a phone book in the same
library) I took the liberty of bowing my head
and running my fingers through my hair. Being
on the lam like mint jelly, I've not been
able to keep up the upkeep on my baroque and
ridiculous beauty regimen, so these pages
are absofaintly covered in my dandruff and
hair. It's a gift from me, OF ME, to you.
And forensic evidence. And DNA. Wouldn't it
be great if after the apocalypse some future
archeologists find this letter in a crum-
bling manila folder and use the DNA to clone
another me? Perhaps I can form the foundation
of a race of slaves for our alien overlords?

Or maybe you'll keep this letter for
yourself. How old are you? What are you
wearing? Do you have a favorite song? Will
you sing it for me? Now?

So, Miii-ISter Laaaaaamber-SON, what
do you think? Prank? Evidence? Are you a
good citizen or a chronic masturbator? Does
my penmanship turn you on? Should I have
included a pair of panties? (Sorry, they
only have letter-sized envelopes here in the
library, otherwise I absolutely would have
sent my DNA in the creepy Internet-nerd-
approved fashion.) Did you throw out the
envelope? Are you contemplating digging it
out of the trash to check the postmark? Or
did that last question grant you a thrilling
moment of superiority because you are indeed
not an enveloper-thrower-outer and you have
it resting on your lap right now, after having already checked the postmark? Good for
you, Miii-ISter Laaaaaamber-SON.

Anyhoo, we are anxious to see whatever you shall do, if the anthrax doesn't get you first!

Yours in Christ,
Julia
PS: Just kidding. We're not all that anxious.

TRANSCRIPT OF INTERVIEW WITH RAYMOND HERNANDEZ, CONDUCTED BY DET. LOUIS ORANGE, HOMICIDE. 5/27/20__.

Q: Did you and your wife ever do drugs?

A. Me? Or my wife.

Q: *And* your wife. But have you ever done drugs? Or your wife?

A: I don't know how to answer that. I think I want a lawyer now.

Q: Why don't you know how to answer the question, Mister Hernandez?

A: Doctor Hernandez.

Q: Doctor, why can't you answer the question?

A: Well, drugs are illegal, aren't they?

Q: Some are. Some are legal with a prescription. But that's not what we're after today. So, any drugs? A little pot, maybe? Ecstasy? Shrooms?

A: No, no not at all. I'm up for tenure. Any dumb thing can count against you, so I've not been partaking.

Q: And Julia?

A: And Julia. God. A month ago it would have been an easy answer. No. Sometimes in the past, but no, I would say no. But now, who knows? Was she doing drugs? Sure, why not. Having an affair? Probably. Was she or had she ever been a member of the Communist Party?

Q: I'll make a note of "No."

A: Okay.

Q: I'll also mark "No" for affair. Is that all right?

A: That would be great, thanks.

Q: Why didn't you call the police when she pulled a gun on you?

A: I was ashamed. I barely even registered the gun. I spent the rest of the night vomiting and calling her cell phone number, but she never picked up. I left so many messages the voice mailbox filled up. I paged her a bunch of times too. I didn't sleep for the next two days; I just kept replaying the last night with her in my head, then the weeks before, the years.

Every dumb argument we ever had. The little comments from mutual friends.

Q: Like what little comments?

A: Anything, everything.

Q: How about an example or two? Little comments about politics? Erratic behavior? Drug use?

A: No, nothing like that. Race—am I too assimilated? Politics. Julia and I had political differences?

Q: What are her politics?

A: Well, I'm a Green, I voted for Nader five times. Julia, she was against most of those votes, thanks to the 2000 election and George W. Bush.

Q: Is that all? Those don't sound like any major marriage problem.

A: No, no that's not all. A week before she left me, I found Julia doing something very strange. Muttering to herself.

Q: Muttering? What was she saying?

A: I don't know. I woke up in the middle of the night and she was muttering to herself. I asked her what she was doing, and she said she was praying. Julia's an atheist. Totally nonspiritual. She didn't even want to go to the Unitarian Universalist Church, not even when some secular event was being held in one. Her parents were religious tourists; they'd been Quakers, Lutherans for a long time, did Shinto for a while. They spent a summer on an ashram in the middle of India, and Julia hated it. One time Julia had come home from school—she must have been ten years old—and her mother had gotten rid of all her dolls and replaced them with faceless corn husk dolls because she had gotten it into her head that Julia was worshipping graven images. Ever since then, Julia has been a hardcore materialist. I would have been less surprised to wake up and see her fellating another man than I was to hear her praying.

Q: What was she praying for? Did she say?

A: I was too afraid to ask. She stopped muttering though, and turned over so her back was to me, and that was it.

6

WE were able to find Julia with some ease though both the police and the media were dumbfounded by her ability to make a public appearance and then vanish. Julia was conspicuous by her absence in the pulsing grid of economic transactions: no credit card use, no flashing of identification or signing a thick book to check into an old, out-of-the-way, hotel. She made friends, sometimes with her wit and sometimes with her sex, and stayed in beds and on couches. She took commuter rails when she could, buying tickets on the train with cash while wearing a wig, babushka, and sunglasses the size of a pair of satellite dishes.

Julia's face was huge on the tabloids; at train stations and bus depots she'd often hold up a copy of the *New York Post* so that her wild-eyed image was staring past the border of the page at Julia herself and pointedly tell the newsstand worker, "I'll buy *this* paper, thank you," but newsstand workers only rarely look up, programmed as they are just to quickly glide a hand across the counter in response to the sound of two quarters hitting the surface. Except for those newsstand workers of indeterminate ethnicity who worked for us.

Thanks to a confusion born of racism, a number of descriptions of Julia faxed to various police departments, security firms, and federal law enforcement agencies described Julia as Hispanic with dark hair and brown eyes, based on her married name. Julia was difficult to spot. When reality contradicted documentation, documentation was followed to the letter, both literally and metaphorically.

Once Julia was nearly captured by an eager police officer in Trenton, as she waited for the SEPTA connection to Philadelphia. He was an older man, with a chin that would have made him a film star in his youth, if only he had an agent who believed in him and apple boxes to stand on so as to be as tall as Joan Fontaine. His stomach gurgled loudly as he moved toward her, old muscles tensed for the first time in years. Something other than directions to the restrooms and rousing the same four homeless people every day from the chewed-up benches meant only for ticketed passengers. Wallace didn't remember that Julia was supposed to be Hispanic; he got his news from the fanned-out array of newspapers with their splashy headlines and photos, not from the official documents he was faxed on a biweekly basis.

Julia was peering out the meshed window down at the tracks below and eating one Corn Nut at a time. She didn't turn to glance at the cop or even register his approach with a twitch or a nerve, a sure sign of guilt and preparation. The officer, his name was Wallace, considered his truncheon. How would that look? She was armed, but one limb was looped around the handles of her purse and holding the Corn Nuts. The other up and tilted at the wrist like a swan's neck to its head, two long fingers digging into the crinkling baggie.

"Ma'am," Wallace said. "Come with me, please." He looked over her shoulder, saw himself in the glass of the window. She was a head taller than he was, chewing with the left side of her mouth. She smiled.

"No," Julia said. "Wallace."

He took her elbow and widened his stance. She was thin, rangy. A hammerlock might do. *Crazy bitches go for the eyes.* That might have been the only quotable he remembered from police academy, decades ago, when women weren't allowed to be police and wouldn't get upset.

"Don't confuse me saying 'please' with this being a request," Wallace said. His right hand took her right wrist. He had control of the purse this way.

"Did you know," Julia said calmly, "that standing pain-compliance holds only work when the person in one is operating under the cultural imperative that one should not attack police officers because they might get shot or charged with assaulting an officer?" Then she dropped her weight and moved quick to the right, then the left. Wallace spun on the ball of his foot to secure the hold, then Julia darted left, straightening her arm. Her feet were between his legs now. Corn Nuts sprayed everywhere. Wallace felt a tug on his belt and quickly moved to secure his gun, but Julia was just looking for a lever as she spun again, her grip on his back and his right elbow. Then the whole train station went sideways and Wallace's head filled with stars. The world smelled like pepper and his eyes and skin began to burn and the world shouted, "Daaaaaamn!"

Wallace doesn't even have an email address, and he types with two fingers, tongue out by the corner of his mouth. A colleague, some toothpick of a boy named Rivera showed him what happened on the palm-sized screen of an iPhone down at the precinct. "See, this is where she snaked out," he said, playing the security camera footage again. Rivera pressed a picture of a button that worked just like a real button and the footage inched forward. "And this is how she threw you. Looks like *Hane Goshi* to me, don't you think? Then she grabbed your Mace and hosed you down, boss." Wallace had no comment. Rivera concluded by noting that judo "is really bad-ass" and that the footage he'd just shown Wallace was "all over the Internet now," even though it hadn't really made the TV for some reason.

Wallace was relieved from depot duty the next day and sent to the local library to deal with the homeless problem there—homeless men tend to hog the public computer terminals and view pornography all day between naps amidst the stacks. One of the computers there used the jerky black-and-white security footage of his encounter with Julia as a screensaver. The head librarian blamed "some kids."

★　★　★

JULIA resurfaced in Greenwich Village after looping around New Jersey and Pennsylvania through means we could not perceive. We saw her in the Ninth Street PATH Station, interviewing two members of the National Guard.

"What are you here for?" she asked them. Julia's appearance had changed again. She had shaved her head, wore little round glasses and a sweeping orange skirt.

"Terrorists," one of the guardsmen said, bored. The other, a woman stared past Julia to look down the long tunnel into New Jersey.

"Terrorists in the PATH Station? "

"Yeah. Interstate transport, you know. Good target."

"So you're here," Julia said, "to stop terrorists with your little . . ." she waved a hand at the guns slung over the shoulders of both soldiers. "AK-47s?"

The female guardsman snorted at that. "If these were AKs, there'd be more trouble than terrorists. That's a Soviet gun. Commies taking over the subway!"

Julia ignored her, keeping her attention on the male of the pair. "So, if terrorists came down here, what would you do?"

"Whatever needed to be done," he said. "Whatever it takes."

"I mean, what I'm asking is this: we're here in a long tube. Did you know that the PATH system used to be called the Hudson Tubes?"

"Yeah, I mean no. It's a tube, obviously," he said, "but I'm from upstate, not here. Plattsburgh.

"Well, we're in a tube here. A long metal and concrete tube that's full of commuters."

"Good place for a terrorist to plant a bomb," said the woman, though she still wouldn't look at Julia. "They used to have trash cans down there, but they took them out. Security risk. So now if someone wants to try something, they have to do it themselves, in person."

"Well then, what set of terrorist problems are you really capable of solving. You're going to open fire on a terrorist if one shows up?"

"If need be," said the woman. "We're mostly a deterrent," said the man.

"Won't you just end up shooting at a bunch of commuters too?"

"If need be," said the woman. "We're mostly here to make the commuters feel better about using the trains."

"If you shoot at them, will they still feel better?"

"Not the ones caught in the crossfire," said the woman. "But the people here the next day, I'll bet they feel safer."

"Maybe it'll take a week or two. Any more questions?" It was hot in the PATH tunnels. Men smelled like small groups after five minutes. He'd been on shift for two hours.

"Those guns aren't even loaded, are they?" The expression on the faces of the two guards was enough. "How about a picture!" Julia said. She pulled a cell phone from her purse and slipped between the soldiers. They obliged with smiles, and the female guardsman even doffed her cap. Julia emailed the photo to Raymond, but it was intercepted by the FBI and put through the graphical ringer—hair added back, skin examined minutely for pore size and cosmetic usage to be cross-indexed with fast food consumption and wireless chatter about women who observe women applying the wrong kind of eye shadow (keywords: "clown college," "whorish")—before being sent on to its final destination, where it broke Raymond's heart.

We spiders do not read minds. We observe, very closely. Raymond saw the email and blanched. He seethed and clenched his fists in the few seconds the image took to load. He turned away and then turned back. Raymond lurched for his mouse to delete the email, but stopped to closely examine the others in the photo, keeping his eyes off Julia. Was she sleeping with the man in the photo? The woman? He muttered, "Who are you fucking now?"

Raymond recognized the PATH station thanks to its distinctive turnstiles and low arch of a tunnel. "Is she living in Jersey?" Raymond paced across his small apartment, subvocalizing conversations he'd never have. Not just the whys and how-could-yous but the conversations they should have had about couples therapy and his mother and getting out of the city.

"We should have moved to Ohio," Raymond said to himself. "So what if it's all one big hicksville? They have the *New York Times* on the newsstands by 6 a.m., Starbucks, a fucking mansion for a grand a month if you want it. We could have had kids . . ."

"Then she wouldn't have left me. Couldn't have. Culturally. Neurobiologically. Fuck, fuck, fuck," he said, interrupting himself. Bile rose and burned his tongue and cheeks. Raymond spent a day in a loop of subvocalizations about subvocalizations, cursing Julia and then himself for cursing Julia and then cursing Julia for treating him so poorly and so cavalierly that he loathed himself enough to curse himself. And every hollow-voiced utterance was punctuated with a loud, resigned, "Cunt."

After a smelly day and night of stewing in his own grief and rage, Raymond left his apartment. He was followed by a plainclothes police officer for several blocks until that officer was intercepted by a man of indeterminate ethnicity who had begun harassing a carefully chosen white woman. Raymond was then able to walk without official observation, except for us. To the Starbucks he went, because it calmed him, knowing exactly what his experience would be like: the smell of burnt coffee, the particular squeal of the pleather couch again his back, Paul McCartney's woebegone face peering forth from CD cases, the deep sighs and explosions of fingers skittering over keyboards from the customers, and himself, already in there stooped over a grande no-whip half-fat macchiato.

Raymond found himself waiting in line behind Alysse, who was trying to pass counterfeit currency to the barista.

"Listen," Alysse said, her hood of her powder blue sweat jacket up around her head, "why would anyone counterfeit dollar bills?" She wore sunglasses too.

"It just doesn't look real," said the barista, a plump girl with a frown and a question in her voice. Raymond looked for a nametag and realized for the first time that Starbucks employees are all anonymous, to be better interchangeable. For the sake of expediency in our narrative, let us call this particular barista "Madison." "And you have so many of them." There were nearly twenty singles in Alysse's hand; Madison's palms were up and wavering, as if someone had just mentioned ringworm.

"Let's put it this way; if you were a counterfeiter, wouldn't you make twenties? Or hundreds? Why bother with ones?" Alysse said.

"I'm getting my manager," said Madison. The line of customers hissed like a snake. Alysse quivered, suddenly seeming nervous.

"What are you getting?" Raymond asked. "I'll just pay for it."

Alysse turned to Raymond and smiled, "Lemon bundt cake." Raymond hmmphed and handed the barista a twenty, "Take it all out of this."

"Let's sit together," Alysse said, putting half the cake in her mouth and walking to a pair of chairs before Raymond could answer.

"You are dressed, I couldn't help noticing," said Raymond, "like the Unabomber."

Alysse finished her cake quickly, and licked a sliver of frosting from her thumb. "I know you. You're on the news. My boyfriend has blogged about you."

"Where did you get those counterfeit one-dollar bills? They were blue."

"Do you want one? They cost a dollar."

"How can one turn a profit like that?"

Alysse smiled. "Volume." Then she said, "What was she like?"

Raymond's insides twisted, then collapsed. "Are you a police officer?" he asked, likely thinking it sounded witty. His face was an off-white sheet, lips tight in what he guessed might look like a smile.

Alysse laughed. "I met her once, just a week or so before the shooting. She's really changed things."

"I really don't want to talk about Julia," Raymond says. He looked into his coffee cup. "I have no idea what happened, but it's all just tragic. No, not even tragic. It's wretched. *Wretchedness* is the only word I can think of." He looked closely at Alysse, who actually closed her eyes while peering back at him, letting her sunglasses do the work.

"Where do you think she is right now?" she asked.

"New Jersey," Raymond says. "I have an email. I didn't bother sending it to the police. I'm sure they've tapped my phones, are monitoring the computer, are following me everywhere"—he stopped to raise his cup in a salute to one of the men of indeterminate ethnicity in which we ride, and we returned the gesture with a practiced chin-up nod of acknowledgment—"and I'm the victim."

"Not too many men can say they've been left at gunpoint, I suppose. Wretched, that is the perfect word for it," Alysse said. "Or for something."

"Did you enjoy your cake?" Raymond said, the way a wall might. He was sitting on his own leg, and it was falling asleep.

"I did. Never been here before."

"This Starbucks?"

"Any Starbucks. I don't even drink hot liquids. I prefer to shop local, or in union shops, and buy direct trade, not so-called"—she raised her hands and twitched her fingers like quotation marks—"'fair trade.' But I was walking by and decided to come in. I wanted to try it out. Luckily, they had lemon bundt cake."

"Most people hate the lemon bundt cake," Raymond told her.

"Ever try it?"

"Er . . . no."

"Well, I tried something new today," Alysse said. "Maybe you should too."

Raymond stirred and blushed. He took a sip of his

beverage and said, "Women are a mystery to me. I admit it. You came here, to this Starbucks, to try something new and just happened to bring along obviously phony bills to try to pass. Why did you come here instead of the Starbucks across the street?"

Alysse said, "I came here for you."

"I'm beginning to wonder if there's something in the water. You sound very much like my wife," Raymond said. "Except that where she was tantalizing, you tend to be somewhat tedious except when compared to the rest of Starbucks's clientele."

Alysse chewed on the last handful of her cake hurriedly. Raymond smiled. "It's not nice to be made fun of, is it?" Then he made a move as if to pat Alysse on the knee, but stopped short, his hand hovering in the air. "Anyone can tear something down. There's no heroism in that, especially in a society that is already fairly dynamic. Perhaps too dynamic. One day you have to grow up. I know there are few rites of passage these days; so many people not wanting families, no real opportunity for lifetime employment or even lifetime careers, but whatever little kooky thing you're trying here, know that you are failing."

"Did you want kids?" Alysse asked. "Did Julia not want kids?"

We didn't hear the answer as we were called away. Many of us were called from our posts, in our men of indeterminate ethnicity, as we had found Julia. Her error was involving herself in the war.

7

JULIA couldn't get into Fort Dix, or over to the Middle East or Central Asia. Wherever there is an imaginary dotted line striping the curve of the Earth, we are there. Travel to Jersey City, however, was entirely within her capabilities. It's a smallish city, more an appendix to Manhattan than anything like an entity unto itself, or even a part of the greater Garden State. Jersey City was built without a center, on swamp and slabs of bedrock, designed to be plundered by generations of minor thugs running herd over successive waves of immigrants. As New York City overheated, the lands over the brown Hudson were filled with the little men and women who served as the teeth in the gears of the economy. On the water taxi between the Financial District and the lip of New Jersey, Julia made a friend in Drew Schnell.

He was easy to spot, Drew Schnell. He kept his nametag—DREW SCHNELL, BONY—clipped to his shirt on the ride home and ate two hot dogs at a time, one in each hand, taking a bite from the right and then one from the left. Hair didn't quite cascade down his shoulders but rather oozed in the manner of something industrial. Julia sat down next to him, and looked at him, and smiled. She said, "Bony?" which Drew Schnell was not.

"Bank of New York," Drew said after a careful swallow. "What do you want?"

"Sorry."

"You're attractive and started a conversation with me."

"Ah," Julia said. "You're suspicious."

"I've taken this water taxi every spring and summer

Friday—a little treat for myself, you know—for three years. Not one person, man or woman, has ever spoken to me, except to say 'Excuse me, please.' And that was on 9/11, when the taxi was the only way back to Jersey with the towers collapsing. It was very crowded that day. So I know that you're not striking up a conversation because you want to flirt. You're striking up a conversation because you want something." He glanced down. "Our knees aren't touching."

"What's your job at the Bank of New York?" Julia said.

Drew smirked. "I'm the reason it takes three days for your check to clear. I collect the money, lend it out for, you know, a day or three, and then collect the tiny amount of interest accrued over the length of the float." Julia said nothing in response, so Drew waited and then said, "It's a volume business. We do about forty-five, sixty mil a day."

"What's your annual salary?"

"Thirty-five K."

"So, you make your year's income in the first ten minutes or so, of the first day of the year, and everything else is just gravy for the bank."

Drew shrugged.

"Oh, please, health insurance?"

"I have nine fillings," Drew said.

"How about a bite of that hot dog," Julia said. Drew turned his right wrist and proffered to Julia the unbitten end of the frankfurter. Relish glistened under the sun. She took a bite. Drew shifted his hips and moved his thigh to hers.

"So, what do you want?"

"Weff," Julia said with a mouthful of hot dog. "I fanth ymm tu gib mfnn t frq."

Drew looked out across the bow, first to the squat buildings of Elizabeth and the growing skyline of Jersey City, then back over his shoulder toward Manhattan. Wind pushed a strand of hair into his mouth. "Fuck it. Okay."

Julia, we know as we have observed her talking with her mouth full a number of times, said "Well, I want you to give Manhattan the finger." Drew Schnell heard, "Well,

I want you to give money to Iraq." And so the next morning, Drew logged into his workstation at the Bank of New York and did just that. Four hundred million dollars, sent to seventeen different concerns, all located in Iraq and held by Iraqi nationals or exiles waiting in nearby Kuwait, without a moment's concerns about security or protecting himself. Drew Schnell was lucky that a janitor of indeterminate ethnicity intercepted him on the way to the restroom and secreted him in the utility tunnels built under the Bank of New York's headquarters. This is what he told us:

I haven't had a girlfriend in ten years. On 9/11, nobody even called me to see if I was all right. I took the PATH every day into the city; I was on the last train out before the planes hit and the towers fell. It was that close. And there were no days off for me either. My own bank in Jersey City was closed—they had a sign reading that they were closed "due to circumstances"—and lower Manhattan was frozen up to Canal Street, but we got shipped out to Brooklyn to deal with the tickets that were coming in, from Chase, from foreign, wherever. 'Round the fourteenth I started getting the tickets from people who died in the towers, people I used to talk to on the phone. Doesn't sound like much, but there it is, you know. Some days, those people were the only human beings I'd ever talk to, and that was just for business, just on the phone. We were working till 10:30 p.m. every night. Not a second of overtime pay—we're "professionals"—you know. All the cops and firefighters were treated like heroes, and don't get me wrong, they were, but so were we. Broker-dealer services heroes. Fifteen-hour days for two weeks to keep the economy from collapsing entirely. After that, it was back to the same ol' grind, except for the stupid president fighting the stupid war in Iraq.

I had a lot of arguments with people online about the war in the lead-up to it, and I was right about every single thing. I knew that there were no WMDs. Anyone with a calculator and a little experience with chemistry could figure that out. I knew that we'd be stuck in a quagmire for years too. People are never happy about invasions, no matter who is riding in on the white horse. It was so obvious, but there was nothing anybody could do about it. Or so they thought! Ha!

"We?" we asked.
"You know," Drew said, "us. Duh."
"Us."
"Us. America. You know."
We didn't.
"Where's Julia?" we asked.
"Julia?"
"The woman with whom you shared a hot dog."
"Beats me. I never saw her after that. I asked if we could go out for coffee some time and she laughed and waved her hand like she was introducing me to the city and said 'I live right down there. Come by, anytime.'"

We put him in the Simulacrum for his own safety, and assigned him a lawyer of indeterminate ethnicity to keep the trial in motion indefinitely.

★   ★   ★

We drive buses for the city now. We run the bodegas and the convenience stores. It's our silhouette in the stained glass window of the Coptic church that was once a Freemason lodge, our slumped form under three coats in the Journal Square PATH station, and our arms pushing the floor buffer over pressed marble in the Post Office built for a city presumed to have a more glorious future than it did. When the Grove Street PATH station was struck by an improvised explosive device, some of the bodies in which we ride were dragged from the slag that remained of the train car. We barely escaped with our lives.

The fire department and security forces filled downtown Jersey City, but even better for our purposes were the news media of two states, their trucks and helicopters, swarming the scene. Julia knew to avoid the cameras, to keep out of earshot of the parabolic mics, to keep from the cordons and the watchful eyes of the police. And that's how we found her. She was there, we were sure of it as she always appeared by the chaos of her making when she could (though the proximate perpetrators, two Jordanian nationals living in Jersey City were found over the course of the next three months) but she was on the rim of the panoptimatrix, in the blind spot.

Specifically, she was in the McDonald's across the street from the Grove Street PATH station, attempting to order a Number 2 meal without onions. When we found here, one of us bereft of anything but eight legs and a mission, she was explaining, "This has onions, like the last."

"Okay."

"I would like a Number 2, with no onions," Julia said. She gestured, with the bun in her hand, to the burger sprinkled with slivers of onion. "This has onions."

The manager turned to his left and spoke over his shoulder. "*Número dos, sin cebollas!*" he shouted, and a lilting "*Sí*" drifted back over to the cash register. The manager lifted the burger and with an outstretched arm presented it to the woman who had said *sí*. She nodded toward the other burger, still on the counter by the squat McDonald's cash register. Julia lifted the bun and saw that that burger was free of onions.

"I need them both to have no onions," Julia said. Then we found the cuff of her slacks and crawled to her Achilles tendon, where we bit and poured in all the venom we could. Julia's chin hit the stainless steel countertop hard as she went down.

8

Tʜɪꜱ is how we made Julia disappear.
    Julia.
    "Yah?" She was awake now, albeit groggy and even talking, though her jaw was purple and weighed down by a mass the size of an orange. Her left foot was similarly warped, and kept her from running or leveling her heel on one of us.
    Julia, listen.
    "K..."
    You are no longer to drink Coca-Cola, nor Pepsi-Cola. Royal Crown is your drink.
    "What?" she said, surprised.
    When you're out at a diner or restaurant, you have the monte cristo, not the pancakes. Not the tuna salad sandwich, hold the celery, but the turkey club without the tomatoes.
    "But...," She was awkward, trying to stand. "Diners don't... No Royal Crown."
    You may drink tea.
    "Oh."
    No more Jersey City. You'll live in Brooklyn. No more L train. You'll take only the J, M, or Z. Your phone service will be provided by T-Mobile, not Verizon. You'll watch *American Idol*, not *Survivor*. You'll follow the Mets just enough to have a casual conversation with a potential lover in a bar, not the Knicks. You are Julia Ott again, not Hernandez. Sundresses, not yoga pants. Special K cereal bars for snacks, not Nutri-Grain.
    You'll consider yourself an Independent with strong Democratic leanings, and will admit to voting occasionally

for Republicans if in the Nelson Rockefeller or Olympia Snowe mode. The *U.S. News and World Report*, not *Time*, not *Newsweek*. You'll prefer to be on your side, in a near-fetal position, during the act of physical love. You'll blush again, and cultivate the tick of pinching the flesh above your lip when considering two options that are both somewhat favorable.

We continued the transformation. The movement, actually, away from the world you know and into the world of the Simulacrum. The Simulacrum is not just a precise copy of the world, it is overlaid on your world, like the other half of a chessboard a particular pawn may never cross. It has everything this world does, save *Hymenoepimescis sp.* The Simulacrum is a web of tendencies and notions, the bakery down the block from the one you go to for your bagel. The Simulacrum is the subway stop you watch blur by as you always seem to be on an express train and it's a local stop. The part of town where the fire hydrants are yellow rather than brick red. The ancient city an obscure writer you pretend to have read in translation was born in. It's where rubber comes from, and alpaca blankets, and its people use the Cyrillic alphabet but only due to Stalin.

The Simulacrum is the home of men of indeterminate ethnicity, the men in which we ride. We are *Plesiometa argyra*. The Simulacrum is our haven, our home. We were welcoming Julia into it, to keep the world safe from her, safe from the pupating wasps in her brain and blood. We don't believe in killing except for our own consumption needs, not anymore.

Julia, slowly coming back to herself, asked, "Why?"

You're a danger. You killed a man. You impressed others sufficiently to fund terrorists and to create minor havoc.

"Fishman had it coming. Lots of people have it coming. And I never encouraged anyone to do anything except to express themselves."

You're a victim. You were stung by a wasp, do you remember? It has changed your personality. We can remove the eggs. They'll never develop on a diet of human blood; they need us. Without us, they'll stay within you forever, further warping your mind. We can protect you from the consequences of the decisions they influenced. In time, your peculiar urges should fade. Until then, we can keep you safe. Safe in a place between places.

She was upright now. "Victim? I finally stopped being a victim. For once in my life I did something with my life, of my own free will, without worrying about expectations, or what people were thinking of me, or how happy my parents were or my husband was or my boss was . . ." she trailed off, the rest of her utterance nothing but desperate exhalations.

This is not a negotiation. It is done.

"Why don't you just kill me? Why go through all this nonsense, offer me this laundry list of little changes?"

It never seems to work out in our favor, the killing.

"What do you mean?" Julia said, her voice light and curious again.

When you hear the answer, you will fall asleep. You will awake in a new apartment, in your new life.

"How is that any different than killing me? It's the murder of the self, it's—"

Archduke Ferdinand.

9

Three months later, Julia was a driver's license photo—chin up, strands of hair across her wide forehead, cheekbones washed out in the light of the flash—on the evening news. Six months later, she was a trivia question and the subject of several photocopied zines and abandoned websites, their links slowly dying. The world moved on, the wars ground on, and the movement flickered and died as we had hoped. A footnote in a thesis.

Julia got a new job, working from home on her computer as a customer support representative for a cable television/Internet/telephone company. For eight hours a day she tooled around her basement apartment in Astoria, Queens, handling the occasional phone call or "live" help chat. At work, Julia went by the name *Undrehuh*, which she believed to be the way a call center worker from Indian might say the name Andrea after taking a course in accent reduction. At the end of her work day, she tooled around the neighborhood, enjoying the wine bars and the occasional dance nights, retiring to the many diners for dishes of flaming saganaki and chilled dolmades.

Sometimes Julia wondered if she should have a child, or run off with some man she'd met via the Internet; he wanted to spank her when the dishes weren't done and who expected to be fellated to completion each morning. She wondered about her brother, who lived in Arizona and did something with shale. Julia never thought of Raymond except when someone mentioned Margaret Mead, a circumstance which was fairly rare.

Julia wrote all these thoughts and whimsies down in a private blog that only she, and we, could read. She occasionally dated a man of indeterminate ethnicity, us. We accessed her computer as she slept and, as we gathered from her subvocalizations, dreamed of murder.

She came out to us after seven months of casual dating. Dinner at her place, the first time she tried to cook. "I never cook," she said. "I took a picture of the rice because it came out okay."

"We're sure it'll be great," we said. She smiled at us; Julia liked it when we used what she called the *editorial we*. It seemed European to her. And we remembered not to do it too often.

"Listen," she said. She poured us some wine, and then twice as much for herself. "I really never cook. I mean, I was at the supermarket today and rolled my cart past the frozen food section to the meats. I was confused when I saw the chicken. You know, wrapped in plastic and yellow foam."

"Confused?"

"It's not white. It's pinkish when it's raw. I didn't even realize that, can you believe it? I thought there was something wrong with the chicken."

We took her cue and cut ourselves a piece of chicken and put it into the mouth. There was something wrong with it. Too dry, hardly seasoned at all. She must have just set the oven to an arbitrary temperature and put the chicken breasts, pink and all, in there and let them cook until we came to the door with our flowers and See's Candies, which we had ordered from all the way in San Francisco.

"Then I tried to call my mother on my cell phone. She cooks." Julia shoveled up a forkful of yellow rice, avoiding her own chicken. "She was a pretty good cook. Well, we went out a lot too, when I was a kid."

"What did your mother say?"

"She wasn't home. The phone just rang and rang. No answering machine, no voice mail. She doesn't have a cell either." Julia laughed. "We all grew up that way, but it's hard to imagine now."

"Don't know what you've got till it's been taken from you," we said, knowing that Julia would correct us in that condescending way she enjoyed: Till it's *gone*, Bob. It would also keep her from finishing her thought. "I haven't been able to call my mother and actually get her on the phone for more than a year. She calls me, but I never call her, not and actually get through. It's so strange . . ."

"So, how did you solve the mystery of the pink chicken?"

"An old lady helped me. I guess she saw the look on my face. She asked me what was wrong and I told her I thought all the chicken was bad. She laughed at first, but then she told me that it was all right. And to wash the chicken first, and my hands, to avoid salmonella."

"Good advice and a good meal," we said, raising our glass. We, Julia too, clinked.

Later that night, after a second dinner of braised ribs ordered from a nearby soul food restaurant and a dessert of red velvet cake and port, we engaged in the act of physical love, with Julia straddling us and rocking her hips harshly, her hands grasping and pulling on her nipples. The low ceiling of her apartment always made us a bit fearful that Julia, who enjoyed this sexual position more than any other, would give herself a concussion, and that she might end up in a hospital and be identified. Though morbid, such a line of contemplation helped us blunt the physiological responses of the body in which we rode, extending the act so that Julia could achieve a climax. Frequent non-masturbatory orgasms help the transition into the Simulacrum. Julia was a fairly quiet woman, a whimperer rather than a moaner, but there were other signals of imminence and climax: her tongue cold against our lips, the nail of her fingers digging into our pectoral muscles, a wink and a snarl of her lips as if she'd just closed a kitchen drawer onto her thumb. Then a quick leap off us and to the glass of water she kept at bedside.

"Tell me about your childhood," Julia whispered into our ear, the ear into which we were nestled. The body of indeterminate ethnicity twitched hard, and Julia jerked away from our shoulder.

"Sleep spasm, sorry," we said. "What did you ask?"

Julia yawned. "Never mind," she murmured. "The past is so strange. Everything is. Did you ever think of someone, like an ex-husband or a cousin or an old co-worker and think, 'Wow, was I really ever the person who was with that person, who had those conversations?'"

"Oh yes," we said. "Everyone does, surely. All men contain multitudes of men, no? Women as well, of course." We kissed her.

"Sometimes I stare at the mirror and don't even recognize myself. I read in a magazine once that it's because the mirror reverses everything, so you don't really under-stand what you look like."

"If that's the case," we said, "doesn't that imply that you've actually somehow seen yourself, your face, I mean, as it really is. That would necessarily be from someone else's point of view, wouldn't it?"

One of us was in the corner of the room, resting in a web, peering down at the two slabs of meat and sweat atop the swirl of sheets in the bed. And that is how we could see our man as how he really was, and why we couldn't ever quite understand Julia and the tiny crises she worked herself into.

"I guess it doesn't matter," she sad flatly, and she rolled over, didn't respond to our hand on her buttock, and didn't sleep either. An hour later we said, "You should try to be happy. So few people do. It's no wonder that so few of you succeed."

★　★　★

RAYMOND was attempting to be happy, but the only thing that could make him happy was Julia. He said it several times a day.

Raymond cut his finger with a can opener and said, to himself, "Fuck, I should just kill myself. Julia. Cunt."

Raymond tried to read a journal, but his eyes kept falling from the page. Even the book reviews were too much for him.

Raymond left the house one day, meaning to take the train to Brooklyn and eat at Junior's like he used to as a child, but once on the A train he decided to go north instead and eat at the Junior's Annex in Grand Central Station because the trip was shorter.

Raymond moved the TV into the bedroom so he could watch various court shows from bed. He liked to try to nap during the actual presentation of the case, and force himself to wake up in time to hear the verdict.

Raymond showered, his clothes waiting for him on the seat of the commode. He stepped out and dried himself off, then put on his socks because his feet felt cold. He stepped off the rug and into a puddle, wetting his sock. He slapped his towel over the shower rod and twisted the ends around, reminiscent of the stem of a noose. Then he put on his pants.

Raymond ordered a sandwich from the fancy Cuban sandwich place he liked, though he'd never been inside and didn't even know if the place had a storefront—maybe it was a kitchen with a long table and a dozen machete-wielding chefs with great slabs of beef and fine cheese hanging from hooks, and a fennel-shooting device holstered on every shoulder—and it came with the wrong cheese, and tomatoes too. Raymond picked out the tomatoes, flung them one at a time against the white door of his refrigerator, and lost his appetite.

Raymond went on a date with a graduate student in psychology, Liz was her name. She was a bigger girl, an Australian with a light accent that slipped down one social stratum after two drinks—not really Raymond's type—but she had a very large smile and he was good at making her laugh. He mostly wanted to see her breasts, which were large, and the date was an experiment. Would a woman still want to kiss him? Were his scars so obvious? Liz was a behaviorist, not a relational psychologist, but Raymond was sure that if he could get her shirt off it would prove he was all right. He muttered this to himself while masturbating in the shower. They would eat at Cucina Di Pesce, his "go-to" first-date restaurant from back in his single days. Bars were nearby for drinks harder than wine, and all the useful subway stops were to the west, en route to his apartment. With sufficient conversation and decent weather he could corral a woman to walk right past the N and the R, the 1,2,3 and sometimes even the A, C, and E trains to join him in his apartment.

Raymond leaned forward and puckered his lips. Raymond had ordered linguini, which he knew never to do as long pastas were prone to looking ridiculous hanging from one's mouth, but he wanted to suck. Liz was friendly but turned her full cheek to his mouth at the end of the night. She did text message Raymond as he lay in bed though. **Good Night...** The use of ellipses is always provocative, Raymond knew.

The next week, Raymond mistimed a payment to his credit card. After calling the credit card company, his bank, and the credit card company again, he threw the phone across the four rooms of his railroad apartment. It hit the wall and cracked the plaster, then dropped behind a pile of Julia's clothes Raymond had collected, to bring to the Goodwill. But the pile smelled too much like Julia. Then the phone began to ring, playing the *Green Hornet* theme song. Raymond's pulse nearly kept time.

"Maybe it's Julia." He jogged across the apartment and began to dig. The song ended. The screen on the phone's clamshell cover read **1 MISSED CALL**. It wasn't Julia. Just an 888-number, the cellular service provider itself. Raymond sighed and let the phone drop onto a pair of Julia's old slacks. He closed his eyes and inhaled deeply, trying to relax. Then the phone beeped rudely. Raymond still had **1 MISSED CALL**. Raymond pressed exit, then decided to text

Liz. Liz was right under Julia in his phone.

HELLO...

She texted back: **Hey! How ru??**

Raymond didn't understand. **RUSSIA?** he texted back.

The Green Hornet blared in his hand. The screen read **LIZ.**

"Hello?"

"Ukraine."

They met at Veselka at midnight, over black buckwheat pancakes and pirogues. They talked about the weather. It had been raining earlier that evening and Raymond said that the streets shone black like velveteen, which he had read in a book that Liz had never heard of. Liz appreciated the line and the sentiment.

"Not a lot of sentiment in your field, hmm?" asked Raymond.

Liz smiled wide, an angry smile. "Jealous much?"

"Sorry."

"They say that behavioral psychologists have physics envy. I've found that other social scientists, especially ol' softies like anthros, have behavioral psychology envy."

"Yeah. Why would I want to travel the world, explore the edges of the human experience, and get paid for it, when I can hang out with pigeons all day?" said Raymond.

"We're not all B. F. Skinner, you know. I believe in the mind and mental disorders like anyone else."

"Oh?" Raymond said. "That reminds, me, I have a question."

"Shoot."

"Therapists are themselves in therapy, are they not?"

"Quite so. Certainly when in training to get their PsyD or PhD at the very least. Of course, most of them fully embrace a psychotherapeutic mindset so it is no surprise that they would attempt to deal with their personalities or problems in that way, is it?" Liz said. "You might as a well ask if priests go to church. They're right there, aren't they?"

"Well, what about behaviorists?"

Liz leaned in close, conspiratorially, and said, "Giant pigeon."

Raymond laughed. "What?"

"We all go a see a giant pigeon, twice a week." Liz sat back and held her arms out wide. "He's huge, I tell you. Monstrous. Imagine an ostrich on steroids. And you know what he does?"

"Pecks at your heads?"

Liz clapped once. "Yes. Just so!" And she laughed her wild laugh, which overwhelmed the clatter of forks against plates, and even the whoosh of spring air and jangling bells of the traffic by the front door. "Twice a week, for a fifty-minute hour, whether we need it or not. Perhaps one day it shall even change my behavior." She laughed again.

"You let it all hang out. You're cute when you smile."

"So, r u," she said, enunciating the words like individual letters.

"I am," he said. "Happy."

"How funny you don't get that. Half the students in my lab actually hand in journals and assignments with that lingo. B4. U2. It's horrid, utterly," Liz said.

"I don't have too many large courses; I just do one undergrad a semester, or did. The worst I have got on a paper was from a student who wrote something along the lines of 'And I go, "Whatever."' I had no idea what it meant, but the paper was on existentialist anthropology and the struggle between competing imperatives within a cultural group, so I gave her a B-plus."

"Right," Liz said. "Was the paper about the, you know . . ." she held up her right arm and waved her hand around, the universal symbol for the nameless movement that had continued, at a simmer, since we had moved Julia to the Simulacrum. Students at MIT had just that afternoon used gelatin to create islands in the Charles River, and there they reenacted the many interventions of Caribbean nations by the Great Powers of the eighteenth and nineteenth centuries. Four drowned rather than submit to arrest.

"No, this was before." Raymond zipped himself up with a great inhalation, as if he had the choice never to breathe again.

"What do you think happened to her?" Liz asked. Then she lifted her cup and took a sip. "You'll have to excuse me. I don't believe in small talk or beating around the bush. It's a terrible Americanism, I think. This expectation that everyone is nice to one another, and smiles—even the service personnel in restaurants smile as if they are deliriously happy to receive an order of McNuggets—but nobody gets close to one another. It's intimacy, laminated for your protection."

"I think she committed suicide," Raymond says.

"Really?"

"No." A busboy appeared with a plastic tub and with a nod and mutter collected Raymond's plates and the small jars of maple syrup and jelly. Raymond smiled at him in thanks, then turned back to Liz who was mimicking his smile with her wide mouth. He slumped his shoulders, defeated.

"Oh, buck up," she said. "Listen, do you want a sexual partner?" He stared. "Oh, you're a man. Of course you want a sexual partner. Look, it doesn't matter." She waved again, not symbolizing the moment per se, but Raymond could not help but react as if it were a tell of a bad poker player. She reached into her large purse and pulled out a manila envelope, crinkled and bent.

"Here. I admit I've been very curious about Julia Hernandez." She put the envelope on the table between them, and then dipped into the bag again to remove a stuffed wallet and extract a twenty-dollar bill. "Curious about you as well, I must say, though not in that way. As far as suicide, I doubt it. Watch yourself, though. Text me anytime. And fill out the form, you may find it handy." She stood up, tapped the envelope, and rather inexplicably to Raymond said, "Oh Em Gee." Raymond lifted a hand to wave and Liz, at the door, waved back, but neither said a thing.

Raymond ordered another cup of coffee and opened the envelope. There was a small pencil in it, and a form of several pages. He took up the pencil and began to write.

> Raymond: Call what we just did consultee-centered consultation, call it a date, call it whatever, call me whenever. Fill it out, you can save me the trouble ha-ha!
>
> Content Description and Analysis
>
> Setting: *The restaurant I used to like before gentrification ruined it and all the old waitresses died and were replaced by mail-order brides.*
>
> Participants: *Me, Liz*
>
> Subject of consultation ~~*Me*~~ *Julia*

Manifest Content	Latent Content
Question about therapists seeing therapists	*Wanted to talk about how I should maybe finally see a therapist. I never even got far enough to talk about it. Liz didn't even ask why I asked about therapy.*
Jokes about pigeon-therapists and "pecking"	*Flirting: is "pecking" some sort of phallic symbol or idea that bubbled out of my consciousness, or Liz's?*
Students, texting	*A way to judge suitability as a mate? Dealing with youth, earning income, even linguistic adaptability?*

The movement	It's everywhere, isn't it, these days? At least in this social milieu. I wonder what people in the red states think about it all. It's like reverse tea-bagging.
	I should probably write something here about having written "reverse tea-bagging"—the triumph of heterosexual impulses over postheteronormative rhetorical norms. Maybe I just need to get laid.
Liz asked me if I needed a sexual partner.	Maybe I just need to get laid.
	.
	.
Asked about Julia.	That happened before Liz asking if I wanted a sex partner. Why did I forget this until now? Why doesn't this pencil have an eraser? I think I need a third column for post-event latent content.
	I miss Julia, so I missed Julia.
Julia Julia Julia Julia Julia Julia Julia	Julia Julia Julia Julia Julia Julia Julia

	.

Development Description and Analysis
Relationship building

I think I could be Liz's sexual partner. Maybe we could get high together first. She's a loud woman, busty. Haven't been with many like that. A little KB could take the edge off. It would be like college again; the flipside of the semester, like we were the students again and our professors were distant and doughy old farts we had to appease just once a month with a paper or a test.

Establishing or maintaining rapport

I guess I should text her.

Problem definition

Julia Julia Julia Julia. I'm writing her name over and over like I was a high school girl scribbling down the name of a pop star—or my own name and appending the pop star's surname. I wonder which is more common—potential paper down the line?

No, intellectualizing my problems. But what problem?

Gathering data on what has already transpired or reviewing previous actions

Who generates idea?

Julia

When are consultant ideas offered?

Who knows? On our second date?

How is consultee anxiety reduced?

Good fucking question.

2.4.4. Are pitfalls avoided?

None have been yet.

Sharing information

I don't even know anything about Liz. I wonder what her cup size is. 36 something, definitely.

Generating Interventions

Do I want a sexual partner? Yes, I do.

Supporting Interventions

I should text her when I get home. Not now. She'll come running back and want to see this form.

Follow-up and disengagement—
assumption of responsibility for
outcome

*When I thought "she'll come running back"
I pictured Julia and looked up and hoped
for a moment that she'd be walking by the
windows of the restaurant, but nobody was
there. At all. Strange for the city.*

Process Description

Was this session helpful?

Oh God . . .

What is the current reality for this
consultee regarding this problem?

*What an interesting turn of phrase. "Current
reality."*

What is my ignorance/bias regarding
this problem/situation?

Julia Julia Julia Julia Julia Julia

What "intervention" occurred?

*~~Maybe I'll get laid I hope Liz doesn't ask
for this paper back~~ Fuck it, let her see everything; my thoughts and my crossing out. I
should stand naked before someone again,
somehow.*

Does the consultee still own the
problem and the solution?

Have I ever?

> How, where or when did I go with the flow?

Have I ever?

> Timing errors or opportunities taken?

Maybe I should have walked Liz out, maybe down to the end of the block and then down to the end of the next. My heart's in my throat even writing this, thinking that Julia would walk by somehow and see me with Liz and freak. No, I'd be the one freaking.

> Was I (positively, constructively, and cautiously) opportunistic with confrontive interventions?

I can't help but giggle and think about the "second date" after reading this question.

> What were my errors?
> What did I learn?

Julia Julia Julia Julia Julia Julia

> Did I share the problem?

Did I share anything else?

MARIJUANA. College flings. That big bubble of flesh from those wasps in mama's basement. Raymond puzzled over the assessment form Liz had given him for a long moment, then realized that he had spent all of their first date talking about Julia, telling Liz virtually everything that the newspapers and blogosphere couldn't. How she liked kids but hated babies as they had no personalities but an endless number of drives. That she pledged a sorority and washed out, and that her pledge nickname was "Jew Spot," her boyfriend of the time having been Jewish. (As was that one girl with whom she had had a fling). How she wrote letters on behalf of imprisoned Koreans and Afghanis, but only once or twice a year after Pacifica radio or *The Nation* had really gotten to her. How she would weave these fantasies of taking on whaling ships with Greenpeace but satisfied herself with $100 checks here and there.

Julia had been a part of the same systems of the world, and comfortable there. Just like Raymond was. Now Julia was gone, and Raymond, still enmeshed in the worlds of commerce and sexual stimulation and resource management and primate games, wasn't comfortable at all. He looked around the restaurant, eyes wide, looking for . . . Julia? Escape? Then he tapped a few notes into his Sidekick.

```
BRIEF PSYCHOTIC DISORDER. SIMILAR TO
"AMOK" (MALAY) OR LATAH? (WHO IS COMMAND-
ING HER TO KILL/ACT?) NEW KIND OF CULTURE
LEADS TO NEW KIND OF CULTURALLY-BOUND
PSYCHOSIS?

POSSIBILITY: JULIA NOT SPARK OF MOVEMENT,
BUT TIP OF ICEBERG. NOTICED BECAUSE SHE
IS WOMAN? RARITY: PENIS PANIC/KORO AMONG
WOMEN. WHAT IS PENIS OF POSTMODERN/IN-
FORMATION ECONOMY. INTELLECTUAL/SEMIOTIC
REPRODUCTION?
```

Finally, a busboy of indeterminate ethnicity hit Raymond's feet with his mop twice. Raymond got the hint, paid his part of the bill and a 30 percent tip, and left for home, alone.

10

D REW Schnell was attempting an insanity defense, we decided. Why not blame the wasps for once? Raymond was questioned by Schnell's lawyer: did Julia have any drug connections? An interest in hypnosis? Was she ever recruited by the FBI or CIA?

"What?" Raymond asked.

"It's true," said the lawyer, a man of plastic and calm nerves by the name of Smith. "Exceptional high-schoolers, especially those who achieve high in math and the sciences, often receive birthday cards and the like from various federal law enforcement and intelligence agencies. To start grooming them for possible post-collegiate jobs."

"Did you get one of those when you were a kid?"

Smith winked. Raymond said he doubted that Julia was on the FBI's radar in high school.

The questions continued.

Did Raymond have Julia's "half"? Half of what? Perhaps you can tell me. I don't know.

Was Raymond familiar with role-playing games? Raymond was a boy in the 1970s, of course he was. Did Julia play any of the major massive multi-player games, like *World of Warcraft*? Did she have a character in *Second Life*. No, nothing like that. Why?

"Drew Schnell was quite a powerful and influential figure on some of these games. We thought there might have been some contact between them on one of the . . . virtual worlds." Smith's plastic façade loosened when he said those last two words. The smile he offered seemed less calculated.

"Of course," said Raymond. He had guessed that much from newspaper photos.

Did Julia try to make you do anything? Give money to rogue elements? No. We had no money.

"You live in the West Village, have tenure, four books out, and you have no money?" Smith asked.

"Rent control. Tenure track at CUNY. Four books, with small academic presses. With the royalties I can sock away enough money for a ski trip up to Vermont, by bus, every year and that's about it. Liberals don't believe in money, you know. That's why we all end up in academia. Conservative intellectuals, they become . . . well, lawyers."

"*Tax* lawyers," said Smith. "Investment bankers."

"Yeah, the masters of the universe."

"Exactly."

Smith flagged and wilted, while Raymond was pleased just to have someone being so attentive and so willing to ask about Julia without judging, offering advice, threatening arrest, or teasing him with the tiniest whisper of a promise of sex. Raymond was energized, blooming in the spotlight.

What did Raymond think of . . . Smith waved his hand. The Elgin marbles in the British Museum had been secretly sprayed with syphilis the other day, Raymond said. Penicillin was sufficient to stop any long-term problems, but it was a shame that the plot was discovered when a small girl became symptomatic after visiting the museum. Smith rubbed his nose subconsciously. Raymond smiled and said that he was against violence and vandalism.

"Is there anything else to"—Smith waved his hand again—"except violence and vandalism?"

"Well, there are the performances, the reclaiming of the public sphere. The concrete ironizing of certain policies—"

"Such as?"

"All those actors hired and made up to look like various Senators who started impeachment hearings in a mock-up of the Capitol that was all over the web and even picked up by some TV stations."

Smith shrugged. "Yeah, that wasn't too bad. Anyway—"

"And then they had the Presidential impersonator surrendering to *Star Wars* stormtroopers and apologizing in tears."

"Moving on . . ." Smith stopped. Raymond waited.

"Is there anything you can tell us that you think might be of help in Mr. Schnell's plea."

"Actually, yes," Raymond said. "I've been writing a paper for the past few months, based partially on my own contemplation of Julia. Ever hear of penis panic?"

Smith's mouth hung open for moment. "Let's pretend that I've not, professor. Enlighten me."

"It's a culturally bound mental disorder, a psychosis. Common . . . well, not *common*, but present in Southeast Asia and Africa. Men believe that their penises are shrinking, melting, or retracting back into their abdomens due to a curse or, in some cases, propaganda enemies. Cell phones, Zionists, chemical warfare. It's a social disorder too. Once one man decides that his penis is withering thanks to a sorceress or Israel, he cannot help but complain about it. Then other men start thinking that their penises are shrinking too. Hysteria breaks out. They get together in the streets, these men, and go on rampages, smashing store windows, running through marketplaces, attacking elderly women. It starts local but becomes regional. Sometimes thousands of men fly into penis panics over the course of a few weeks, especially if the local media picks up the story."

Smith said, "I cannot help but be reminded of the Twinkie defense." And then he laughed.

"Anyway, in patriarchal, phallocentric, hierarchal, shame-based societies all the ingredients are there. The penis is infused with immense personal and social power. Men at or near the bottom of the social hierarchy are especially anxious because there are no social safety nets, and there is immense pressure to succeed and substantial entrenched corruption that keeps them at the bottom of the heap.

"Sounds a bit like Drew Schnell to me, doesn't it to you? He has a penis panic, and there was even a phallic exchange of sorts with the hot dog. He probably has some kind of sexual dysfunction, maybe a fetish or two. Hmm, is that right, would you say?"

Smith dipped his head in acknowledgment.

"And he's a clerk. Bob Cratchit working for the world's biggest Scrooge. No wife, no girlfriend, right?"

"Right."

"So there you go."

"Penis panic made Drew Schnell embezzle money and turn it over to the Iraqis, and your wife, who pulled a gun on you the night she left you then killed a man and went into hiding, was the catalyst?" said Smith.

"Right."

"All right, Doctor Hernandez. That should be all," Smith said.

When Raymond got home, there were letters from three refereed journals turning down his paper on the subject of his wife.

☆ ★ ★

DAVAN was working on his novel. Alysse was playing a computer game called *Central Planner* in which the object was to maximize outputs and gulag populations of a wintry mid-twentieth-century country while fighting off imperialism. They sat on the futon, laptops on laps, hair in eyes, their cat Stymie between them.

"Tractors?" asked Alysse.

"Films about tractors."

"Hmm." She typed and clicked.

"Tractors are capital-intensive. Factories, steel mills, rubber, and galvanization. Lots of skilled labor, so hard to coerce too. Movies, on the other hand, they're all chicken wire and *papier-mâché*," Davan said. "You can be like Roger Corman, using stock footage over and over, the same damn tractor for that matter, a Stalin impersonator to play Stalin, public domain musical numbers with revolutionary lyrics, shoot it all in the daylight so lighting isn't a big deal. Crank it out on the cheap and keep the peasants happy."

"And then ship them off the gulag, and they'll think it's Disneyland until they get there."

"The Disneyland of tractors, yes."

The cat saw us. She raised her head so slightly, like a queen.

More typing. "How's your chapter?" Alysse asked.

"Slow."

"You're typing a lot."

"I'm on the Sans Nom bulletin board," Davan said, and he wiggled his hand in representation of the nameless movement. "Got into a stupid flame war with stupid fucking Brian."

"All flame wars are stupid," said Alysse. "But what makes Brian stupid?"

"You mean other than the fact that he abandoned *Williamsburgist* after we wouldn't have a threesome with him and moved to Georgia because his grandma doesn't charge rent?"

"All right, all right. But you can't deny that all flame wars are stupid, and if Brian is stupid for being a pig, then you're not much less stupid for still talking to him"

"You know how difficult it is for me when I see someone who is wrong on the Internet," Davan said. He tilted his laptop toward Alysse, upsetting Stymie, who leapt from the couch and walked toward us. We were near the television, warming ourselves on the vents of the digital converter box. Alysse didn't bother to turn her head away from her own monitor. "It's about whether or not a bulletin board about"—this time he waggled his hand—"is actually part of it, or the objective enemy of the movement. If we sit here and plan things out and talk about them and judge our actions or set limits, then it cannot be part of the movement."

"What about Nazis?" Alysse said absently.

"Godwin's Law!"

Alysse rolled her eyes. "I guess I should stop talking now then."

"Actually, that's part of the flame war too: someone said Nazi, and then we invoked Godwin's law, but he said that Godwin's law only applies if one compares one's rhetorical opponents to Nazis or Hitler. Either way, we didn't want to talk anymore, but then someone else pointed out that Godwin's Law doesn't state that a conversation ends when someone says Nazi, but that all the signal-to-noise ratio just skews all the way to noise."

"Well, if that's the argument now, then Godwin's law is right," Alysse said. "Godwin's law is self-invoking too, isn't it? The second someone invokes it, the real fight is crowded out by Godwin's law, because of its articulation."

"Ouroboros."

"It's all rather head-up-the-ass anyway."

"Dark and wondrous," Davan said. "Like the collective unconscious." He started to type and then he said, "Ooh, I should use that in my book somewhere."

Alysse startled, and then pumped her fist. "Yay! Got my first million!"

"The first million is always the hardest." Davan kissed her cheek.

"Thanks, babe."

The cat pounced.

We lost sight of Alysse and Davan for over an hour. Coincidence, like the wasp *Hymenoepimescis sp.* nearly always militates against us. Indeed, after the cat had jumped upon and consumed one of us, knocking the digital signal converter off its precarious mount of old textbooks and DVD cases, Alysse and Davan lost their Internet connection. Soon enough, the line buzzed in Julia's apartment.

"Hello, this is *Undrehuh*. How may I help you today?" she said.

"Uh, yeah, hi," said Alysse, her voice tinny and distant. "We have a problem with our cable and our cat."

"Well, I'd be pleased to assist you with the cable," Julia said. Then she stepped off script. "Did you say cat?"

"Yes, my cat knocked over the converter box. Now it doesn't work."

Julia led Alysse through the process of power cycling—unplugging everything and leaving it to idle for a minute—and Alysse, being a friendly sort, decided to play a little movement game.

"Yeah, we really need our cable back right away, and the Internet too. Speaking of," she said, though she wasn't speaking of anything, "ever get the feeling that everyone else in the world has free will, but you are a slave to forces beyond your control. Or, how about vice-versa?"

"Afraid I've never thought of either of those."

"Why are you afraid?" Alysse wasn't very good at this sort of thing, which occasionally made her stomp her foot.

"Oh, nothing to be afraid of. At worst we'll send a technician out. Let's power up the converter, then the wireless router, then the laptop, in that order, okay?" Alysse did, and the system did not reboot. Julia, as *Undrehuh*, ran a test signal through the devices and turned up significant packet loss. It was probably a short from our little comrade-self, squashed across the green field of a circuit board.

"It looks like we'll have to get a technician out to you; he'll probably just bring a whole new converter for you."

"Is there anything I can do in the meantime?" Alysse asked. "I pay all my bills through the Internet, have work to do. My boyfriend does graphic design; he talks to clients via IM all day. I mean, what are we supposed to do?"

"Nothing right now, to be honest with you. Nothing I can help you with here. We will credit your account and we'll have someone out in three days at the latest. Is there anything else I can help you with today?"

"Whatever," said Alysse.

"Yahbye," said Julia.

★   ★   ★

WE don't know everything, cannot be absolutely everywhere. If we could, we would have destroyed *Hymenoepimescis sp.* long ago, a genocide unparalleled by human endeavor. Our numbers are considerable but not infinite. We can only assume that "Yahbye" was sufficient for Alysse to make the leap that Julia was still alive, and that she had a job as a telephone service rep. Thankfully, as per the posting she made on a movement message board the next day, from the public library, Alysse was sufficiently confused by Julia's faux accent that she declared that Julia had moved to India. A fundraising party committee was immediately initiated to send Davan and Alysse to Mumbai to find her.

11

T HIS is how Drew Schnell appeared to those outside the Simulacrum.

DUNGEON MASTER: DREW SCHNELL, HOW HE WENT FROM 'QUIET GUY' TO THE NERDMAN OF ALCATRAZ
Scott Schatz | Staff Writer, *Rolling Stone*
Nov 4, 20__

SAN FRANCISCO, CA—Drew Schnell is the type of man who lives alone. The Jersey City financial services worker, age 33, has no wife and had no roommates. His days were spent in the bowels of the Bank of New York, and evenings in a tiny Jersey City efficiency apartment, eating take-out alone, reaching out to a few acquaintances via the Internet, and going to sleep alone. After being implicated in the illegal transfer of hundreds of millions of dollars to Iraqi nationals, many of whom have ties to the continuing insurgent movements, Schnell still lives alone, on waterfront property. Alcatraz Island.

Schnell may be a Homeland Security nightmare, but he was a defense attorney's dream. Schnell is white and a native-born American, apolitical, had no criminal record or ties to extremist groups, and allegedly engaged in what was essentially a nonviolent act of embezzlement. Further, a number of the groups to which Schnell allegedly wired funds were U.S. allies—hardly a way to aid and abet the cause of terror. Were money to be traced back to terror attacks or the insurgency via the Iraqi-American Committee or the Brotherhood for Progressive Islam, it wouldn't only be Schell on the hot seat. The Supreme Court ruled that Schnell would need a trial and could not be held incommunicado at Guantanamo Bay, nor any military prison.

Perhaps to keep up the aura of danger, the federal government developed an alternative for Schnell: Alcatraz National Park was shut down and the tourist attraction transformed into a fortress of solitude for the imprisoned finance professional. Media access to the island, and thus to Schnell, is tightly constrained, but *Rolling Stone* managed an exclusive interview with the latest, lone, and likely last prisoner of "The Rock."

We were given all of ten minutes with Schnell, and due to security concerns Schnell's answered were limited to three words per question. A guard was stationed by a button that cut off the phone connection between this reporter and Schnell after the third word Schnell uttered, regardless of what it was to be or whether the sentence would even be comprehensible from such a sort stem of a statement. Longer utterances, we were told, could be used to transmit messages to terrorists.

Schnell's head is shaved now; the shaggy mop and sideburns behind which he hid his face after his arrest are gone. Around his neck and head he wore a steel halo of the sort sported by victims of traumatic spinal injuries. "To keep him from nodding or shaking his head," we were told. "Only three words," said the guard, warning us as much as him.

Schnell is thinner now as well. We asked him about the food; he answered, "Doesn't agree with." If he said "me," it was cut off by the guard under the three-word rule.

What are his thoughts on America? "F__ them all."

Did he do it? "Call my lawyer."

A countdown mentality could not help but take hold. There were no clocks on the wall, and we were relieved of our watches and cell phones—even the photographer's digital camera and light meter were impounded immediately after one photo was snapped, and returned to us intact on the boat back to San Francisco—the ten minutes may well have been five minutes. It could have been thirteen.

Schnell misses the World Wide Web. He has had no visitors save us and is not allowed correspondence. To pass the time, he looks at Fisherman's Wharf. He is reading the Bhagavad Gita. Schnell is irreligious but chose the Gita as the book he is allowed access to thanks to his First Amendment protections because "it is long."

Robert Dahl, Schnell's lead attorney, is as loquacious as Schnell is brief. Dahl moved his practice from New Jersey to San Francisco to have more regular access to his client. Dahl is not a happy man. "It's torture," he explains. "Keeping him there all by himself is just torture. We saw this with Padilla. The guy was brought out of the brig a broken human being due to isolation, sensory deprivation. The guards don't communicate with my client. They're actually trained in ASL so they can communicate with one another without Drew overhearing."

Dahl has been holding his cards close to his vest as regards his legal strategy. Though rumors have been floated of an insanity defense, attempting to pin the transfers on cyber-terrorists and even the federal government itself, there is little in the way of a legal paper trail. "All in good time, all in good time," Dahl explains. What of his client's precarious mental condition? "I have a plan."

The only legal papers Dahl has filed so far involve a unique legal strategy, to say the least. It's a combination injunction/threat to begin a class action suit against the federal government for depriving Americans of their ability to visit Alcatraz Island as a national park. Dahl isn't interested in damages per se, he literally wants the park reopened, with his client Drew Schnell as the primary tourist attraction.

"Human beings are social animals, it's pure genetics," Dahl told us. "Evolution demands it. The orangutans of Borneo are not social. They couple ever so briefly in the great green canopy of the jungles, and then separate forever. It's a tragedy, those ape mothers and their few children, and the species is one the verge of extinction thanks to that. Lowland gorillas? Sure, I know what you're thinking,"—he didn't—"they're social. Yes, but too hierarchal. A single silverback, making all decisions, killing the infants of their rivals or predecessors. Who needs that? No wonder they're endangered too. We're the great naked ape, *H. sapiens sapiens*, we need to touch, to love, we all must hang together to avoid hanging separately.

"It's a national park, great. Let it be a national park. Let Drew Schnell be the Nerd Man of Alcatraz. People pay their taxes to have this guy tortured, to have Iraqis blown up for ten years plus; shouldn't they get to see it, shouldn't they get a show? In the Constitution, every American is given a right to confront his accusers. Well, check the docket: it's *Schnell v. United States*. How can he confront his accusers, every one of them? Isn't that what freedom is all about?"

Dahl, when he isn't talking, is a bit hard to look at. He's a bland individual, white with a broad face and hair the kind of brown you forget about the second your eyes are off it. His accent is hard to place too; it's strangely clipped though some of the vowels are rounded in the fashion of a Pennsylvania Main Line. He claims to be "from all over," and to have traveled the world. "Yeah, I'm still doing that. New

Jersey was a pit stop. San Francisco is destiny." He often puts a palm over his ear when fielding questions, "to stop the buzzing."

Dahl wants to turn Alcatraz into a panopticon, the famed hypothetical prison designed by philosopher Jeremy Bentham, in which a single guard can observe all prisoners without the prisoners being able to see the guard; the prisoners never know if they are being watched, so act as though they are always under surveillance. Except we'd all take turns being the guard. "It's in our brains. There's science involved," Dahl says as he digs through a folder for a few torn pages from a magazine. It's an old study from 2007, in which the human lab rats were put in a functional MRI and given a computer game to watch. The computer played itself, badly, and this caused the posterior superior temporal cortex, the "empathy center" of the subjects' brains to fire off.

"See? We cannot help ourselves. Way in the back of our brains, where we are still primitives, practically lemurs, we experience empathy, we seek to help. Drew is out on The Rock to keep him out of the public eye, to poison the well against him. He needs to be seen, by as many other people as possible."

Schnell has scattered other allies. Some of the so-called (non-called) *Sans Nom* movement is backing him, albeit in ways that only members of that kooky group can. Several thousand false income tax returns were filed, perhaps a reference to famed Alcatraz inmate Al Capone, but the checks included with the returns had routing numbers that exploited a bug in IRS computers, leading to the nationwide rebate of fourteen cents per taxpayer. Rumors abound that Dahl is also being paid by the movement, which is represented most often by a wave of the hand, but Dahl dismissed those rumors . . . with a wave of his hand.

Then there is the ghost. Like virtually any big old building, Alcatraz is considered "haunted" by the sort of people who consider hauntings a possibility. Schnell is being held in 14D, the famous haunted "hole" in which a convict was supposedly attacked by a "creature" or the "spirit" of another convict. Television psychic Lulu Latif has expressed concern for Schnell's safety and began an online petition to have Schnell moved . . . to another isolation cell in the prison. Schnell, for his part, said "not really ghost." When we asked for clarification, even as the clock was ticking down, he only said "yellow spidery eyes."

If there is a specter haunting Drew Schnell, it may just be the woman he claimed told him to embezzle the funds and remit them to Iraq. The police have found no trace of the woman, whom he says approached him on the ferry he took between his job in Manhattan's financial district and his Jersey City home. Nor do any of the security cameras on the ship or either dock show Schnell talking to a woman, though most of the footage doesn't show Schnell at all. He liked to sit on a bench by the stern that just happens to be in a "blind spot," and on that bench is where his encounter with the mystery woman supposedly took place.

"Damn that bitch," he said during the interview. What does Schnell want? "See her again."

★ ★ ★

WE made a point of showing Julia this article one night when we were over, riding in our local man of indeterminate ethnicity. She didn't recognize herself in the story, or Schnell, and indeed didn't seem very interested in reading the whole piece. The cover, however, was unnerving. It was a photo of Keith Richards, as it so often is on *Rolling*

Stone even after fifty years of publication. Julia spotted the magazine on her coffee table, where we had left it for her to nonchalantly discover, and with a start called out to us (we were in the restroom), "Who is this, the Crypt Keeper? *Fangoria*! Oh . . . never mind. Man, he does not look good."

12

We believed that Raymond often thought of Julia when he engaged in acts of physical love with Liz, despite Liz's different somatotype. He cupped her breasts, which were larger and longer than Julia's, as if they were Julia's, using the same splayed five-finger grip. He thrust his hips into the delta of Liz's thighs with insufficient force to please her—Liz would have to correct him by lifting her legs and planting the bones of her ankles against Raymond's buttocks to push him along. Also, one time he called her Julia and got a slap across the face for it.

Raymond balled up his fist, but let it go and turned away. Liz said she was sorry, casually. "Sorry then," she said.

"I'm the sorry one. In both senses of the word," said Raymond. He shifted to sit with his back against the wall, nearly crushing us.

"Perhaps," Liz said. She slid her palm down her belly, to her pubic mound.

"I can't continue, not right now," Raymond said. "I'm just very bummed out."

"Don't mind me," Liz said in a whisper, and she manipulated her clitoris until she orgasmed, taking several minutes, groaning deeply, her voice like a man's. Raymond licked his lips, not from excitement but perhaps from thirst, but didn't disrupt the proceedings by leaving the bed to fetch a drink. When she concluded, she rubbed her fingers together and then ran them across the roll of Raymond's belly, leaving his skin slick and hair smeared and stuck to his flesh.

"I just don't understand it," Raymond said. "It's been a year and every day is still a hammer being slammed around the inside of my skull. So many associations, so much baggage. I can't listen to the radio because I hear songs Julia liked, or lyrics that sound like something she said once, or might have said. Movies are impossible; the smell of the popcorn, the red velvet seats, they're our early dates, ghosts hanging in the projector light."

"And when your penis is in some woman's vagina, it reminds you of her as well," Liz said. "Yes, I understand." Raymond said nothing, his lips stretched thin with potential retorts. Liz swung her legs off the bed and stood, her back to Raymond. "I'm quite annoyed with you, you know. The name was just half of it. Really, a gentleman would have at least lent a hand, even if he wasn't up for it anymore, if you get my meaning."

"You're obsessed too," Raymond said. "That's why you're here, with me. Wasn't your last boyfriend an French-Canadian lifeguard whose only knowledge of English was his phonetic memory of Metallica lyrics?"

Liz slipped on her panties, and her blouse, but did not button it. Instead, she reached for her cigarettes and withdrew one from the pack with her lips, put the pack down to pick up the lighter, and lit up. Raymond scowled. "Those'll kill you," he said, "and will annoy me for three weeks." He coughed meaningfully.

"Your rooms smell like Julia and anxious sweat," Liz said. She exhaled smoke through her nostrils, two streams swirling into a great cloud before her. "Let this be a nice set of associations written into your autonomic nervous system. Smell smoke when walking past a bar, you think of fucking me now." She raised her arms and shook her breasts at him.

"Instead of zeroing in on that sweet beery smell and thinking of me and Julia at the Holiday Lounge on St. Mark's, with all the old guys muttering into their gins."

"Good enough." She sat back down on the bed, her butt half off, her legs straight and knees locked. Then she tilted backwards and peered up at Raymond. She made the glow of the cigarette pulse. Finally Raymond moved from the wall and lay down next to her, both figures across the short side of the bed.

"Do you think she's sane again, wherever she is?" Raymond said. "In India."

"If she's in India, I certainly hope not."

Raymond tsked. "That sounds borderline racist. There's nothing wrong with India."

"There's *nothing* wrong with India?" Liz repeated.

"If Julia is sane, I'm sure she's cosmopolitan enough to deal with the cultural chasms she may need to navigate. There's certainly nothing wrong with many of the urban centers of India that she couldn't be able to handle had her faculties returned to her."

"You get many rewards from the notion that Julia was mad."

"You get plenty from the idea that there is no such thing as madness, or for that matter notions," said Raymond. "It's easy to do whatever you want and treat people however you like if you consider them all, and yourself, behavior-making machines zipping around the countryside, eating stimuli and shitting responses."

Liz sucked deeply on her cigarette. "Touché," she said finally.

"A new insight to have the pigeon peck out of your brain this Wednesday."

"I only hope he can get it all without giving me a migraine." Liz said. Then they rested against one another, Raymond's lungs grumbling as he held in a cough.

"Though, you know, there are plenty behavior-making machines out there," Liz said. "Rats infected with toxo-plasma will seek out rather than avoid the smell of cat urine. The protozoa within their wee brains drive them to present themselves to be eaten, for only in a cat can *toxoplasma gondii* sexually reproduce."

"Protozoa sexually reproduce?"

"These do. But only in cats. Elsewise, they just produce

pseudocysts in the intermediary hosts. Pregnant women so infected may give birth to schizophrenic offspring."

"You believe in schizophrenia?"

"It's easier than not believing in it, these days."

"I wonder if Julia's mother had a cat."

Liz leaned up and extinguished her cigarette, then turned to the right and straddled Raymond. He stiffened under her, as did his member. He smiled and grabbed her hips, then lifted his head and torso to bite her left nipple.

"Let's make some behavior," he said. His penis did not retract, nor did it cause him to panic.

Several hours later, after Liz left for the evening, Raymond had a craving for a sort of doughnut he didn't often buy. He went to the Food Emporium, which was a twenty-four hour supermarket, and there he saw Julia. He went home and paced his small apartment for hours, gnawing on his fingers till they bled.

13

Raymond saw Julia several times and, indeed, also saw one of us again. We were at St. Mark's Bookstore on a sultry summer night, poking around the zine section, on our knees peering at merchandise near the bottom of the shelving unit. Zines, especially in these days of the Internet, are the near-exclusive precinct of the extremely observant and/or psychotic. Raymond was neither, and nearly tripped over our broad back.

"Oh, hmm, sorry," he said. His arms were full of books from the bargain tables. Deviant sciences—the dream machine, orgone boxes—in luridly scholarly trade paperback. We stood and smiled at him. We liked him. Still do, indeed.

"No need to apologize," we said. "You have to expect that kind of thing when on the floor."

"Expect?"

"Kicked. When you're down."

Raymond's expression grew dark. "I don't think I'd say *kicked*."

We smiled at him. "Then there is a need to apologize, my own. Sorry. For everything." Then we sunk back down to look back at the zines.

"Excuse me," Raymond said. "This may seem like a strange question . . ." he trailed off and we looked up at him. "Where are you from?"

"Oh, all over. Heinz 57, you know." We decided not to act offended, though in St. Mark's Bookshop a thundering condemnation of the political implications and ingrained privileges of such a question would have certainly been acceptable.

"No. I mean, do you live in the Village?"

"Oh no," we said, and we took the opportunity presented by another patron squeezing between ourselves and Raymond to stand up and back away from him. It was an unnerving experience, feeling Raymond's eyes upon on as we walked past him into the center of the store to pretend to peruse the coffee table books—perhaps that itch is what you all feel when you see a spider walking down a white bedroom wall. We rode our man of indeterminate ethnicity out of the store and let others keep an eye on Raymond.

Raymond came home with his books and set them on his worktable. He put on his work glasses, turned on his work lamp and got out his purple and green stickies and yellow highlighting pen. Two minutes later, after attempting to read the first few pages of each of the books, then resorting to skimming to study the diagrams for the construction of a dream machine and an orgone box, he gave up. He turned on his laptop, found an ambient iTunes radio station he liked, and drank three fingers of vodka from a dirty glass in his sink. He texted Liz—**R U THR?** and then checked his phone every few minutes, setting the ringer volume all the way up, all the way down, and then all the way up again to make sure it was working. He poured himself another vodka and then fell asleep, face-down, on his couch. His ankles hung off the side.

It was nearly 3 a.m. when Raymond awoke. *The Green Hornet* was playing, louder than usual. He'd turned up the volume. Raymond lurched off the couch and grabbed the cell phone, not bothering to check the display before he answered. "Yes, hello!" he said, nervous.

"Who is this?" the voice on the other end demanded.

"You called me."

"My name is Lamberson."

Raymond squinted in the dark to find the time. The cable box had it. "It's three in the morning. Look, if this is one of those dumb movement things, include me out."

"I hired a private eye to find you, and this number. Julia Hernandez's husband." The word husband hit Raymond like a rock. He nearly spasmed. "And yeah, I agree, include me out. Your wife ruined my fucking life. Cops, IRS audit, constant questioning, my neighbors and poor mother too. Those damn kids and their stupid spectacles. Cameras on my lawn constantly, and spiders everywhere. I've been up for three days, working up the courage to call you."

"Oh, *that* Lamberson. Well, you got me, what do you want?"

"*Bubble Yum* has spider eggs in it," Lamberson said. Then Raymond heard what sounded just like a gun being fired. He laughed. It sounded almost too real, as if the cell phone hadn't warped the blast as it must warp all sounds, as if the peaks and dips of the frequency-bundle weren't sliced free by the digital speaker. "Fucking idiot," he said. He hung up and waited for a call back.

Then Raymond called back and the phone rang and went to voice mail. Then Raymond wrote down Lamberson's number as it was recorded by his phone, muttered his thanks to God that it wasn't just labeled "Private Call," called the police and told a sleepy officer what had happened. He fell back to sleep and was awoken again at 7 a.m. by the first media inquiry of his long, long day.

Lamberson's suicide brought Julia back into the media eye, and Raymond as well. The latter was easy enough to deal with—a reporter of indeterminate ethnicity met Raymond in the freight elevator he took in the hope of avoiding the media while on his way to his office at City College, and asked him about his theory of penis panic and how it related to his ex-wife. Raymond was pleased to look into the camera as if giving a lecture and sketch out his theory: a psychologist (he did not mention Liz) may diagnose Julia with brief psychotic disorder, but the ragged band of followers that emerged in the wake of her murder of Fishman suggests a culturally bounded phenomenon.

Penis panic happens across much of the developing world, where men are anxious about their historically superior position in the culture. In a culture where everyone is depositioned, one need not have a penis in order to panic. Indeed, having a penis is rather an obstacle to panicking . . . except in Lamberson's case. He then apologized to and expressed sympathy for Lamberson's family, as he too knew what it was like to lose something. Some*one*, someone, he corrected himself. Not something. Then he looked away from the camera and down at himself.

Once the video hit YouTube, several moments later, nobody was interested in talking *to* Raymond anymore. The video of him took his place, became him in the media ecology. "Penis Guy" was a very popular search item for several days, and Raymond's video even managed to crawl to the top of the heap within, breaking through the thick clouds of the pornosphere.

Julia we made ill with sufficient venom to keep her bedridden and delirious. She would lose weight, perhaps lose some hair, not be the hard-eyed woman in the grainy license photos or the dancing blur turning Fishman's head into a fountain of purplish-red on three different cell phone videos, but someone else again, weak and bent over like the defeated heroine of a short story after her miscarriage and a husband's affair with a first-year co-ed.

Who we missed was Liz. Liz who felt for Raymond, much the same as we did and do, and who wished to please him. She let herself in to his apartment with a plan to make some dinner, but she saw the books and was inspired. She went down to the streets and bought a disused phonograph machine and a long tubular lampshade of the sort Westerners read as Oriental, and used Raymond's work lamp for the light source. Our little body in the little room felt that quake within, the quake we feel when *Hymenoepimescis sp.* begins to work within us. The drive to build a warped and twisted web, not for ourselves, but for the horrid asocial *other*, the beast that is nothing but a machine of reproduction and slaveries, and the fear that that body has turned against us, that we spin our own suicide, that is what we felt.

And Liz, who is never graceful and not very handy, but also not squeamish, crushed us before we could bite her, before we could stop her. This thirteenth chapter, so unlucky for us.

14

W E do not know, but we can assume, that Raymond's late rebuff of the normal run of social and natural sciences was due to the rejection of his penis panic thesis. Further, we may conclude that perhaps he had read a few novels in his day, and remembered some connection between *latah*, *amok*, and *koro*—those culturally bound disorders of the anxiety and the lash—and the pseudosciences of the mid-twentieth century. We can guess that when Raymond climbed the three stories to his apartment and was both relieved and aggrieved that no news crews were waiting for him, he did what he would normally do: put the key in the top lock and unlock it, then put his second key in the door lock and unlock that, then withdraw the keys and hold them between the fingers of a clenched fist as he nudged the door open with his shoulder. This is what he'd learned to do when the city was unsafe, and what he still did decades after it had become a landscape laminated for his protection.

And he opened the door not to his usual ramshackle order, but to slices of light painting orbits along the wall, to the dream machine grinding away and Liz peering into it with slit eyes and a twist of lips. And he kicked the door shut with his heel and kept the keys in his fist so they would not jingle, and he sat down on the kitchen floor and joined her.

There, on the floor—and this is just induction, mind you—he began to understand. Julia, the Julia of his mind and body who was nothing but a doll made of knotted complaints and betrayals, unraveled. A madwoman, a murderess, an amoeba on the slide. There are no uncaused actions, so what might have caused the change in her behavior? What caused the change in his behavior? The woman across from him, Liz, was both cause and effect, as was the dream machine. As was Julia. His mind gave way to the machine and its cycles of spin. There was a machine, he sensed, causing Julia, just as the machine in front of him was causing himself, causing Liz.

Liz. Yes, yes. What was it Liz said? Rats that don't fear cats. Little specks of life and urge within them change their behaviors. Was Julia pregnant, or could she ever have been? Thick with his seed? No, the idea was repugnant, it felt wrong in his mouth like a tomato on the verge of turning rotten. Something else. Stung by a wasp. Then, we do know that Raymond opened his mouth to say something to Liz, but instead he jerked, spasmed, and slammed his mandibles onto his tongue as the brain completed its circuit and triggered an episode of photosensitive epilepsy. Liz was up and at his side immediately, forcing Raymond's jaw open. She kicked the phonograph's power cord out of receptacle, sending the whole contrivance tilting to the side. She held Raymond's head close to her breast and muttered something to him. In a few seconds it was over. He opened his eyes in time to see us drifting down our silks, our shadow the size of a fist against the wall.

"Are you all right?" Liz asked, carefully annunciating each word, trying to fill Raymond's vision with her mouth.

"No . . . ," he said softly, his tongue hurting. Then he just waved her away, his gesture so reminiscent of the gesture surrounding the movement. He tried to get up, using Liz as a brace but couldn't until she stood and heaved. He took the two steps to the fridge and wrote on the small whiteboard on the door, "LONG ISLAND."

"What? You're going to Long Island? Your mother, yes? But now?" Liz said. Raymond pointed to his pained mouth in response and shrugged apologetically. He said "wasp," but it came out "vizzp." He went to write on the board again but dismissed it and led Liz by the hand to his bedroom. On the laptop he did a few quick Google searches on *wasp* and *alter behavior* and eventually came up with a popular article about a scientific study of our plight: *Hymenoepimescis sp.* and its parasitic methodology for reproduction. It enslaves us, makes us spin a web-cum-abattoir for their pupating offspring. We build our own gallows for the sake of the murderer's child.

Raymond's tongue was feeling better, well enough for short sentences anyway. "Remember, Julia?"

"Wasp, yes. She was bit by one, I remember. But these wasps are Latin American and they don't affect humans," Liz said.

"Latin American things can find their way north," Raymond said. "And maybe they do affect humans."

Liz shrugged. "Anything's possible, I suppose. We don't know much about parasitic neuromodulators."

"Or the human mind. I had a mystical experience with the machine. It all came to me."

"Mystical experience is it!" Liz snorted.

"I've had them before, just never in my house. Or in the U.S.. Anyway, this is what happened to Julia. She was doing something, something big, setting up some set of circumstance—"

"For the benefit of the wasps?"

"Who knows? Maybe it's just bad programming. What happens if you try to run a Windows program on the Mac operating system?"

"Nothing, Raymond," Liz said. "In the overwhelming majority of cases, nothing happens. Apple and Microsoft make sure of it, after all. It's a matter of design."

"And nature," said Raymond, "isn't a matter of design. Look, it's also something else. I've seen Julia."

Liz just raised an eyebrow and folded her arms across her chest. "In the flicker?" she said finally.

"On the streets. Here and there. Looking different, acting different, but still her. As if she were in the witness protection program."

"And the wasps did that as well, hmm?"

"Probably not," Raymond said. "That can just be a coincidence. Maybe Fishman was a mob guy. Probably was, anyway. I can find out though; I just need to find the wasps and find Julia."

"And I just need to finish my thesis by the morning and entirely revolutionize the way we conceive of behavior and the mind, and then we can all stop thinking about economics or sociology or ethics because I'll have it all sorted," said Liz. "I mean, surely your mother would have called an exterminator, and if the authorities could not find Julia—"

"The authorities could be the ones hiding Julia," Raymond said.

"Be that as it may, how are you going to do it?"

"Let's set up the dream machine again. I'll clench a spoon between my teeth in case of troubles again."

"I think I'll go home instead, Raymond." She stood up and walked out of the room with purpose. From the kitchen she called back to Raymond, "Don't let me stand in the way of you reuniting with your wife." The door slammed.

15

THE next morning, Raymond went looking, not for Julia, but for Alysse. He went to the Starbucks where he had encountered her before, presuming that she was a regular and would need a coffee before work, but she was not there. He asked a barista if she was a regular—"You know, short girl, elfin features, boyish haircut?"—but the barista, who shared many of those features, was wary of giving an older man with brown skin and well-chewed lips information about a young female. Raymond didn't realize how he must have looked to the barista until the same strategy failed with the nearly identical barista at the Starbucks across the street. Then Raymond remembered that Alysse had told him that her boyfriend had blogged about him. His Blackberry was sufficient—not too many eyewitnesses had blogged about the shooting as it was more of a "Twitter thing" (as Raymond mumbled to himself even as he ran his search) and Williamsburgist.com came right up. So too did a scan of an early anti-Fishbowl flyer with what was obviously a home phone number belonging to "Davan and Alysse."

Forty minutes later, Davan buzzed someone into the building and waited to see who it was behind the open but still chained door to his apartment. "Holy shit!" he said too loudly when he saw the top of Raymond's head. He nearly shut the door, but Raymond peered up the well of the steps and shouted, "Please, wait!" and ran the last three flights.

"Davan," Raymond said. "Is that right?"

"Yeah," said Davan. "Uh, come in." The door shut, then opened again. "Please."

The apartment was tinier than Raymond's, and crammed with books spilling from milk crate bookshelves and spools of well-insulated cable littering the floor. Davan picked his way past some of the junk and Raymond followed as if stepping in new snow. The apartment smelled of supermarket doughnuts. "Alysse, better get out here!"

Alysse opened a door that appeared to be for a closet. "Oh!" she said brightly when she saw Raymond. "Hey."

"Listen," said Raymond, "I've been rehearsing what I want to say for the entire subway ride, and I still don't know what quite to say, or to ask, but I need help. I even rehearsed this part. And saying that I rehearsed this—"

Davan put a hand up in front of Raymond's face, "I've been stuck in one of those rhetorical loops myself. Just take a second to reboot. Want a hard lemonade?"

"I want to find Julia. She's my wife."

"Who doesn't want to find her?" said Alysse.

"Lots of people, I'm sure," said Davan.

Raymond looked around for a place to sit. Alysse sat on the coffee table, moving a laptop aside with an expert bump of her hip. She patted a space next to her and Raymond gingerly sat down next to her.

"We think she's in India," said Alysse.

"I've seen her several times in New York. Recently."

"I've talked to her on the phone. She was working in a call center in Bangalore, I'm sure of it. She was faking an Indian accent."

"Well," said Davan, "why would she need to fake an Indian accent in India?"

"You're just starting that again because you think he'll—" Alysse said, nodding with her head towards Raymond, "agree with you."

"Forget India for the moment. Or don't. Has Sans Nom ever tried to locate Julia?"

Alysse twisted her hand in the air, both the reference to the movement and a way of expressing indeterminacy. "Yeah. Kind of. We put up videos—"

"Hacked Julia Roberts's bank accounts—"

"We were planning something for July. Dunno what it is yet."

"Well, I have an idea. Why not just go around knocking on doors?" said Raymond.

"Like Jehovah's Witnesses?" Alysse asked.

"Yes. Or campaign fundraisers. Mormons. Trick-or-treaters."

"That's totally random," Davan said.

"So you'll do it?" Raymond said. "Even though it might actually work?"

"Yeah, sure." Alysse picked up her laptop and opened it on her lap. "We'll get right on it."

"Okay, thanks," said Raymond. He stood up. "I have to go. This is just one stop. Things are going to change now. I can feel it."

"Are you going to knock on doors on your way down to the street?" Davan said.

"Should I?"

Davan peered at Raymond meaningfully.

"Okay, I will," Raymond said, but when we walked down the steps he didn't bother knocking on even a single door.

16

STONY Brook is the second-to-last stop of the Port
Jefferson Long Island Railroad line. On weekdays, in
the mid-afternoons, few people other than train conductors
and unfortunate nap-takers make the entire trip. Raymond
did, however, to visit his mother and, he hoped, the wasp nest
in the basement. There was simply not enough humanity for
us to blend with, so we could not send a man of indeterminate
ethnicity to track him, to stop him. *Plesiometa argyra* followed
along, to let us know when Raymond would be returning.

We met Raymond on the way back to New York City,
joining him as he transferred at Jamaica to the LIRR train
to Penn Station. Though the train was somewhat crowded,
the passengers gave Raymond a wide berth as he was
carrying a heavy wooden box from which issued occasional
flapping and buzzing sounds.

"Hello, Raymond," we said, sitting down across from him.

"Do you have Julia?" he asked the man of indeterminate ethnicity.

"She doesn't want to hear from you, and truly you
don't want to hear from her. She's safe. She's enjoying her
life. If you find her, then what? The authorities would seize
her and arrest her for murder. She'd be imprisoned, perhaps
institutionalized, perhaps even executed."

"Or maybe she'd be put on display on Alcatraz, eh?"
said Raymond. We chuckled as his comment was an invita-
tion to do so.

"So, who are you?"

"We oppose the expansion of *Hymenoepimescis sp.*
populations out of their native habitat."

"Department of Agriculture?"

We had a cover story planned. It was not necessarily an excellent one, but it would have done sufficiently well to lower his guard—he'd pressure us and we would agree to allow him to meet Julia. We would have shuffled him off into the Simulacrum, and tossed the box in the East River. However, the box was not a very strong one and a wasp escaped. We were stung.

Our man with indeterminate ethnicity tried to hold it together but could not. He burped and twitched and I, hanging from the ceiling, felt my blood burn inside me. Then it all made sense again.

"I'll be honest with you," I told Raymond. "Those wasps warp human history. Akhenaten! Zhuangzi! Napoleon was a victim, Hitler as well. For the *Plesiometa argyra*, it's fine. Not fine, nothing like that. It kills us; you've read that, I know. We've been spying. *Plesiometa argyra*, that's us. This form you see is something we make, a cocoon of sorts if you will, controlled by the collective intelligence of hundreds of thousands of spiders. You see, we chart the course of world events; we are everywhere or mostly so anyway." Raymond was looking perplexed so I grabbed him by the shoulders and shook him. "You have to understand, this is all for your own good. It's us and only us standing between you and total war, endless genocides, a charnel house world!"

The guy who looks funny starts messing with Ray and his box with the wasps and there's a pain in my back and I want to spin a big ol' square thing and rest and sleep drifting and dreaming on the train yeah and then Raymond gets up and my guy gets up too and grabs him and then Raymond does this judo move and a lady starts shouting but most people are just really into their newspapers and iPods but a couple guys are standing and shouting for Raymond to kick that guy's ass and Raymond is all

frea_{ked}

OUT

cuz he's gotta

he **gotta**

the ARM he's got my guy's arm all twisted in his hands that Raymond didn't believe a thing till the arm starts to untwist and melt into webbing and the train is about to stop and here comes the conductor

so

I
d
r
o
p

the rim of the
on
hat

and crawl inna his
eyes

AND BITE BITE BITE

17

THANKS to the disincorporation of a man of indeterminate ethnicity and the swollen face of the conductor one of our number attacked, Raymond was able to flee the train when it stopped briefly and the doors opened. The police were far more interested in the conflicting reports of assault and a sudden spectacular explosion of spiders crawling on the walls and chairs of a train car to care much about a man, even a Latino, who pushed back when pushed.

Coincidence tends to conspire against us, though it is the nature of coincidence to be mercurial. The stop at which Raymond quickly exited was Kew Gardens, a neighborhood of the Simulacrum. There are no Starbucks in Kew Gardens, no Quiznos Subs. It's an ethnic swim of Indians, Africans, Orthodox Jews, Latins from three continents, and those oiled and tanned airline workers who are always on their way to or from JFK or LaGuardia airports. They are us, and just one method via which we cover the world. Men and women, all of indeterminate ethnicity, all taking notice of Raymond as he wandered the streets, as he looked for another way back to Manhattan.

Raymond was cagey by now, and in shock from the episode. He could only walk three blocks, then make a right turn, then try three more blocks, and make a left. We smiled at him as he passed, trying to be reassuring. We did not want him to open the box in which he kept the wasp nest, we did not want to hurt him anymore. Nor did we want him to be stung. The wasps in his box were a generation younger than the one that had infected Julia, and perhaps further mutated for it. What if one stung him?

We wanted to apologize, but we did not think he could handle it.

Plesiometa argyra is not organically a social animal, at least not according to human taxonomy. Ironically, *Hymenoepimescis sp.* is social, as most wasps are. Yet, our secret evolution has led to an *ur*-sociability; we were intelligent as a collective when men were still lemurs holding on to branches and blinking in confusion at the jungle nights. We created our first men of indeterminate ethnicity when the Cro-Magnon rose up against the Neanderthal and in the confusion of genocidal war slipped into the population.

Hymenoepimescis sp., social in their primitive and mechanical way, never developed intelligence. And still they preyed upon us, as innumerable microorganisms prey upon you, as *toxoplasma gondii* and other neuromodulators push and prod you in minor ways. *Hymenoepimescis sp.* is rare and the mix of social conditions, individual genetics, and psychological propensity leading to the creation of disruptive elements is rarer still, but the impact on history and life itself is so profound that we cannot risk even a single exposure. We had to bring Raymond in to the Simulacrum. We needed Julia as a lure.

Her boyfriend of indeterminate ethnicity was dispatched to her house, while a cable technician was dispatched to the telephone pole at the end of the block to end her workday and give her a reason for a picnic with a beau.

"Kew Gardens," she said when we arrived with a basket of food procured from a supermarket. "Isn't that where all those people stood by and watched while someone stabbed and strangled that girl?"

"Kitty Genovese was decades ago," we said. "You weren't even born then."

"Things change, I guess," she said. So we went.

Kew Gardens is still fairly green despite being packed with residents living in row houses and older apartment complexes, though the only useful place for a picnic is by the Maple Grove Cemetery, which is where we led

Julia. For Raymond and his fatal box of *Hymenoepimescis sp.*, his route toward us was easy enough to arrange. A bus stalled across two lanes of Metropolitan Avenue, snarling the way for taxis. A man of indeterminate ethnicity helpfully gave Raymond long and tedious directions to a subway station, which we then shut down by reactivating the old public toilets that were long ago shut down and sealed behind a wall of plaster and tile. The flooding led the MTA employee on duty—not one of us, but she may as well have been—to flip the circuit breaker that powered the MetroCard machines and close the entrance gate. Raymond encountered a subway station that only allowed for egress, and moved on.

As we suspected he would, Raymond decided to head for high ground, a trick he learned in the field amongst the gitanos of Spain. From a high point, he might be able to see another subway station, or a taxi stand, or a bud, and even if the views were blocked by buildings and other construction (which they are in Kew Gardens these days), he might meet someone who could give him more helpful directions along the way. The hill even gave him a way to orient himself—most helpful locations would either be "up" from where he was, or "down." We lost track of him in the streets a number of times, as the *Plesiometa argyra* must keep their distance.

We sat with Julia on a strip of grass under a tree and along the iron fence of Maple Grove. The traffic that day was light—another advantage of the bus cordon we had contrived a mile down the road—and there was little in the way of either noise or exhaust to disrupt our meal of salami and tomato sandwiches, chicken with blueberry chutney, and clear sodas from a local boutique bottler (cream and orange). Raymond was walking slowly, almost at a shuffle and his shirt was stained with sweat. He held the box in front of him as if it smelled, his bare arms trembling.

"Raymond," said Julia blandly.

Raymond looked over at us and then his knees buckled, his flesh suddenly white.

"Do *not* drop the box!" we called out, and he stiffened again, yanking the box toward his stomach to cradle it.

"Raymond, what's the matter?" She turned to me. "It's been so long, I . . ."

We stood up and walked past where she was sitting. "It's *latah*, a stress response. He'll obey," we told her. "Raymond, come here!" and Raymond walked up to us. His eyes were huge and oily. Julia was up right behind us with a bottle of water. "Put the box down gently and take the water," we told him and he followed both commands. "Drink." He did. "It's a common enough phenomenon amongst you . . . amongst some people. In circumstances of extreme stress, people will simply comply with any shouted order."

"Raymond, Raymond . . ." Julia had never forgotten him, or her old life. They were just distant, like the names of junior high school teachers all but forgotten.

"Don't you want to come with us?" we said to Raymond. He stared at us for a long moment, his skin like wet ivory and his cheeks puffed as if he were going to vomit. He opened his mouth. There was a living *Hymenoepimescis sp.* on his tongue. Then it flew at our man.

☆　☆　☆

JULIA was not comfortable in her old apartment. She stood, hugging herself and scratching. She'd taken a bath and changed into an old robe, one she remembered loving, she told Raymond, but it did not feel like something she should be wearing.

"I have money, you know. I secreted some away." She looked at the box containing the *Hymenoepimescis sp.* nest. Next to it sat an ashtray in which she and Raymond had lit half a pack of cigarettes; the smoke they hoped would sedate the wasps. "When did you start smoking anyway?"

"I can't stand smoke," Raymond said, his throat raw. "It's from . . . a friend."

"We can't stay here."

"I know," said Raymond. "Is this what life is like on the run? Every moment a white knuckle?" He glanced at the door again. "Every footfall in the hall. God, I was so nervous that my cell phone would ring when I had that wasp in my mouth. I'm sure Mister Hamm down the hall will smell all the smoke from the cigarettes and knock on the door, and if we don't answer, call the fire department. Did you see how that guy you were with just"—he waved his arms a bit—"collapsed into webby goo?"

"I don't know what it's like to be on the run." Julia let her robe fall open a bit. "As far as I knew, I wasn't on the run. Everything just resolved itself. I was a different person." She scratched her shoulder. "I can't believe I lived like this," she said.

"It's paranoid-making, yeah," said Raymond.

"No, I mean in this apartment," Julia said. She nodded at the top of the refrigerator, "With that selection of tea." She tugged on the lapels of her robe. "With this type of clothing. I mean, I'm not even the slightest bit attracted to you. No attraction, no affection. You're not even my *type*, Raymond. I can remember being with you, smiling when I'd wake up and you were there next to me, but I can't *feel* it. It's how they hid me. They changed every little habit and opinion I had and I just fell off the grid."

"Oh."

Raymond made himself some tea. "They're not even human. They're constructs. Were you having sex with that thing? Was it platonic?" he asked, mostly addressing his teakettle.

"We were close."

Raymond shook his head, disgusted. "I spent a year crying over you. I was so excited when I saw you with that guy. That . . . whatever. I put a wasp in my mouth for you, I could barely stay conscious, but I knew what could happen." He sat on the edge of the coffee table, his back to Julia. "What *are* they?"

"Spiders. In a war against wasps," said Julia. "They told me things."

"Me too. Culture and society, all of modernity is apparently an epiphenomenon of the occasional wasp who stings a person instead of a spider, in the right circumstances."

"And the spiders want to tamp it all down; it's better for them if society is stagnant."

Raymond turned, "Stagnant or stable? Let's not forget that you went from a good person to—"

Julia was up, her body in Raymond's face. He had to stare. "To *what!*" she said. "Nothing's changed. I am a good person."

"Everything's changed, Julia. You left me. You killed someone. I met another wax man before the one from this afternoon. That sting was an accident. He went crazy, spilled the beans about everything. Hitler was apparently a sting victim. Who knows how else?"

"I left you, so I'm Hitler now?"

"No, you killed someone so you're not a good person."

"You killed someone too," Julia said. "Bob."

"He wasn't a person," Raymond said, "He was a wax dummy. God knows what."

"He was a sentient being," Julia said. "What's the definition of human: 'Not full of intelligent spiders'?"

Raymond nodded emphatically. "Yes, well. Yeah. Pretty much by the definition of the word human, spiders in a man suit are disqualified. Christ, Julia. What the hell? What the holy blue fuck is coming out of your mouth?"

Julia sat back down, lowered her head and started to cry. "Gawd."

"Maybe he's not even dead. Bob," Raymond said. "*Bob,*" he said a second time, spitting it out. "Like termites building a mound; there needs to be a critical mass of intelligence to create the mound, otherwise they have no idea what to do. I'd hug you now Julia, but I don't think you want that."

"You're right," she said, then she sobbed again. "What do you want, Raymond?"

Raymond sipped his tea. He blew across the surface of the cup as well, even though the tea was cool. He took another sip. "My life has been ruined in every way. My marriage. I'm probably a wanted man by now; aiding and abetting a wanted killer and fugitive. And my life's work has gone to shit. It's all been solved, hasn't it? Human cultures are an artifact of parasitic neuromodulators; we have no free will, there's no real cultural evolution that isn't ultimately exogenous, no relevance perhaps to our material cultures. We may as well be amoebae on a slide."

"Are you having an existential crisis too, Raymond?" Julia asked. She wiped her eyes with the thick and floppy sleeve of her robe.

"Yes. I may as well just erase my hard drive and stick my head in the box. I mean, I was going to try to find someone in the bio department to take a look, to try to figure out what was going on, but it hardly matters. If you have your gun hidden somewhere, just fucking shoot me."

"It wouldn't help," Julia said. "That's why the spiders didn't kill me. You can't just crush the Brazilian butterfly whose flapping wings whip up the monsoons in Bangladesh."

"You end up melting the polar ice caps instead."

"Pretty much. That's why I was, you know, *removed,* for lack of a better word. From the world, from the person I thought I was."

"Only *thought* you were? You mean the Julia I fell in love with or the Julia who pulled a gun on me and shot Peter Neads Fishman?"

Julia opened her mouth to answer but stopped as there was a knock on the door. Raymond and Julia exchanged glares, but Julia just shrugged.

"Who is it?" Raymond called out. The deadbolt answered by turning over.

"The landlord?" Julia said.

"Or Liz."

"Who?"

Liz opened the door. "Who is it?" she said. "Some welcome." She turned to Julia. "I seem to have won the prize." Then she sniffed. "My cigs. Did you miss me so much, Raymond?" Back to Julia. "Close your robe, dearie. Your vagina will catch cold."

Julia said, "Hello." Raymond looked at his feet and blushed, as red now as he had been white just a few hours previously.

"We've been looking for you all afternoon, you know. Sans Nom. Knocking on doors all over the world."

"You're in . . ." Raymond wiggled his hand.

"Who isn't?"

"I'm not," said Julia.

"Nor me."

"Our loss, I'm sure," said Liz. "What's in the box?"

"Human nature," Raymond said.

★   ★   ★

WE had a thought: *Kill them all.* Though our last act of murder led to the Great War, the stakes were high. Our careful machinations over the course of millennia were not self-interested, or not entirely self-interested. We do want to reveal ourselves, to join together with humanity, to form a society of two intelligences, two species who cooperate rather than compete for environmental niches. Unfortunately, humanity is not ready, thanks partially to *Hymenoepimescis sp.*, partially due to your own deeply ingrained antipathy toward arachnids. Let us assure you that, until recently, the feeling was mutual. Only after thirty thousand years of living amongst you in our men and women of indeterminate identity, of living parallel to you in the Simulacrum, have we come to appreciate *Homo sapiens sapiens*—your tiny broods and overindulgence of your young, your diverse material constructions, and the creativity of your religions. Our prodding and pushing, our protection of the species as a whole from the worst instincts of those ethical outliers that nearly inevitably seek power, our compassion for the plight of your starving bottom billion and the personal agonies you all go through due to the wax and wane of endogenous opioids, catecholamines, and neuropeptides—the chemicals of love and madness—we are slowly making you ready. We are nearly done. Another eight thousand years, perhaps. Know that your nuclear arms do not work. Know that "peak oil" will undermine global warming. Some of your descendents will live, and will be psychologically and anthropologically adapted for the revelation of our existence.

Like *Homo sapiens sapiens*, we occasionally have urges that go beyond the needs to feed. To murder rather than cull. It passed, and our singular envoy hanging from a silk on the wall of the apartment hadn't the venom to disable all three humans. There was little the trio could do anyway, though they did try.

18

Liz insisted they take the long walk uptown and then across the island to the United Nations. "It'll give us more time to argue about how insipid this all is," she said. "Further, they clearly have the trains if they found you on the Long Island Railroad."

"Yeah, we had a lot of traffic problems today in Queens too. We had to get a cab to Astoria and then come back into the city," Julia said. "Raymond, dig out the old cooler so we can carry the box in it. It'll be another layer of protection, and look less conspicuous."

Raymond obeyed without comment, but Liz had one, "So you'll walk into the General Assembly with beer, is that it? They'll let you right in if you're claiming to pass out lager. Well, except for the Muslim countries, I'm sure. Clearly, nobody in history has ever been so clever."

Raymond came back with an empty cooler; it was blue with a white top and handles, and about three feet on its longest side.

"We never did get to do any picnicking," said Julia. "I went today, of course. I wonder how Bob knew."

Raymond sighed and looked up at the corner of the room where in the intersection of two walls and the ceiling we sat watching and listening. "Spiders. They're everywhere. I'm tempted to open the box." He reached for the box containing the nest of *Hymenoepimescis sp.* "See, it's scuttling away now. That's how. They're everywhere."

Liz reached from the broom behind the refrigerator and took a hearty whack at the webbing, but we had already fallen back.

"We never got an exterminator in here either. Twenty-five hundred a month for a railroad apartment," said Julia, "and we may as well have been living in a college dorm."

"Did Bob spray often?" Raymond said.

"Of course he did."

"Surely given his, its, their—whatever!—issue with wasps, he would," Liz said. "It was just a coincidence that he had the attributes of your dream beau."

"Should we be talking about this in the same room as a spider?"

"You sound like a paranoid schizophrenic," Liz said.

"It's been a hard day," Raymond said.

"I have to get dressed," said Julia. "Are the rest of my clothes where I left them?"

"Of course they are," Liz said.

Raymond busied himself with wiping the interior of the cooler with a washcloth from the kitchen sink and placing the nest of *Hymenoepimescis sp.* within.

On the streets, Julia and Raymond carried the cooler between them, each holding a handle. Liz circled them as the walked, sometimes in front, walking backwards to better harangue them and other times shuffling immediately behind them, her knees knocking into the cooler.

"I thought you were in Sans Nom," Raymond said. "Isn't this sort of gesture what you're all about?"

"No," Liz and Julia said together.

Liz wiggled her hand. "It's not about getting killed. It's about finding the flaws in the design, the weaknesses in the structure, so they might be exploited. All the wacky shenanigans are just an initial phase."

"It's about pushing things forward," said Julia. "It's sort of inane to complain that deviance isn't pro-social in the short term."

"Whose side are you on anyway, Julia?"

"I don't know."

The group stopped in Union Square; Raymond and Julia needed to rest their hands and everyone wanted

Starbucks—"I only take Starbucks when there are two choices available." The Barnes & Noble at the top of the Square had one, and there was also a coffee shop on the Western end of the square, roughly one hundred yards away from the bookstore. Julia sat on the cooler and refused to move, so Raymond chose the store on the surface, the better to keep an eye on his ex-wife. "I'm not staying with her," Liz said as she followed Raymond.

In line for their drinks, Liz said, "Is there any particular reason you are going along with this nonsense. I mean, other than the fact that you're still in love with a woman who left you at gunpoint. It's just your ingrained responses to seeing her. The heart leaping from your ribcage, the dry mouth—"

"My mouth isn't dry."

"Yes it is. That's why you're getting a fancy little soda instead of your usual macchiato."

"Everyone's such an accomplished detective these days," Raymond said. He paid for his drink, and for Liz's and a fistful of biscotti.

"You're a creature of habit, love," Liz said. "And your love is a psychotic creature, I should remind you."

"Not anymore. And that's for both of us. Trust me, there's nothing I'd rather do than go home and write a paper about this and maybe end up being interviewed in the *New York Times* for my controversial new theory of social behavior, but I . . ." he trailed off and put the bottle to his mouth. He crossed the street briskly, nearly leaving Liz behind; she was on her phone after it chirped to signal receipt of a new message. Julia was still on the cooler, sitting with her knees together and feet splayed, chin in her hands.

"Goddamn pataphysics," Raymond said. "Let's go,"

Cutting north into Gramercy, where the buildings were tastefully ornate and the chains gave way to boutiques, Raymond told Liz, "Let's say you quit smoking." Liz responded by sliding a thin cigarette from the pack she kept in her left pocket as if she were a man, and lighting it with the lighter from her right. "You'd have a craving for a cigarette."

"Of course."

"How would you eliminate those cravings?"

"I'd have a bleeding cigarette."

Julia laughed. "Ha! That wouldn't eliminate your cravings at all, just postpone them through temporary satisfaction. You'd eliminate your cravings only by not indulging."

"How can I live a normal life?" Raymond asked. "Simple; make sure that everyone knows what's been going on, in no uncertain terms. Expose these things in a way that cannot be denied by any reasonable person. Create a new normal." He turned to Liz, "Settle the question, once and for all. If anthropology is a solved problem then I can get on with my life. Without this, no way."

"So it's about you then, not the greater good or hunger for knowledge?" Liz asked. "Physics envy as a solution to penis panic, eh?"

"He's not the only party here," Julia said. "You can address me occasionally if you'd like to. I am holding half the cooler here."

Liz exhaled a swirl of smoke. "Maybe I should just wave down the next police officer I see." She pulled out her cell phone again and thumbed some keys.

"Put it down," Raymond said and he and Julia both lowered the cooler. He stepped up to Liz, getting in her personal space, his eyes squinting from the sting of smoke. "I'd like you to assume that the narrative we presented before is right."

Liz nodded, "All right then."

"If the narrative—that there is a second intelligent species on this planet, one that is actually a prey species to a parasitic neuromodulator. Further, at least in some cases, humanity is a prey species to this neuromodulator, and this has had a significant impact on philosophy, culture, history, and geopolitics, and until this afternoon there was nothing in the historical record to suggest that this is the case.

"Further, the other intelligent species in question also manipulates the course of world events, perhaps even informing them in a way as profound as neuromodulation apparently does. This other species has managed to hide itself completely, while presenting some level of existence as an unintelligent arachnid. And yet, for all their intellect and apparent resources, they are still ultimately a prey species. They tend to predominate only because they reproduce in the manner of arachnids and thus can swamp out much of the impact of the wasps.

"What this means is that of all the people—hell, all the sentient beings—in the world, the billions of us, there are a very small number of organisms with free will. In fact, by my count, there are two. You're one of them."

"And me?" Julia asked. But then she deflated. "Ah, the wasps, yes. I have to say . . . I felt free. When I stole money, did graffiti, killed Fishman. But all those things seem so trivial, just stating it all at once now. Is it really any different than any other vandalism, or theft, or . . . you know?"

"Yes," Raymond said, "I'd say it was. It was different because while your behavior was being influenced by some other organism, it was *not* being influenced by the spiders, but rather by the wasps. It's antinomian praxis, after a fashion, which is why those actions had a much greater impact than they might otherwise. Anyway, excuse me, I'm getting knocked off track—" he turned back to Liz. "There are two organisms on this planet with sufficient information to actually realize that the social context in which they are existing, the *thrownness* of it all. I'm one, you're two. That's it. Everyone else has strings on their wrists, ankles, and jaws. That's why I need your help, Liz. Please, I just want your half."

Liz exploded in laughter. "Well what can I say! To not act is an action as well, if you believe farty old Nazis like Heidegger." She raised her foot and extinguished her cigarette on the heel of her boot. "And yet, Ray-Ray, I have to ask, how do I know that you have free will? Perhaps the spiders fed you misinformation. Perhaps when you had that wasp in your mouth, all as part of your daring plan to save Julia here from a life of middle-class tedium slightly different than the one she had with you a year ago, it stung you, or another one did? Perhaps you were stung on Long Island, or a year ago? Maybe there was a sexual transmission of whatever chemicals informed Julia's escapades—"she nodded to Julia and interjected, "no offense," into her own monologue. "So, she's a marionette with another master, Raymond. Well, perhaps you are too in your own way. Indeed, the only person who I can be sure has free will is myself."

"Well, then I need you even more," said Raymond.

"Let's keep walking," said Liz.

Raymond kissed Liz on the cheek. A chorus of horns and shouts blasted forth from Third Avenue as Julia dove bodily into the street.

"Julia!" Raymond screamed, and he ran after her, but Liz intercepted him with her strong arms. "No!" she said, just as a bus steamed to a stop right in Raymond's path. The bus driver screamed curses, muted by the thick wide windows of the bus, and waved his arms violently, which was plain enough. Raymond crudely shouldered Liz out of the way and kicked the side of the bus, then waved his arms and mouthed curses, knowing that it would be futile to bother raising his voice. The bus lurched forward several inches but stopped again as Raymond cut in front of it and walked into the evening snarl of traffic. Julia was gone.

19

W E lost track of Julia as profoundly as did Raymond and Liz. Raymond walked back, ignoring the honk of horns and the polyglot imprecations of the cabbies and commuters. "This doesn't change a thing," he told Liz. Liz took up the cooler handle that had previously been Julia's and continued the march.

"Double-time it, eh?" said Liz. "Who knows if we've attracted the attention of the police."

"You haven't been living in New York long, have you?"

"Yeah yeah. Nothing's more tedious than an intellectual posing as a badass because he lives in a very nice area in a city that used to have rough areas. So, how shall we penetrate the United Nations?"

"Honestly, I was kind of hoping that something would happen that would allow us free entry."

Liz stopped. Raymond walked ahead till he felt his cooler handle nearly twist away from him. "That's your plan?"

"Planning isn't possible. Surely you can see that. We have to improvise. Really, I thought you might be able to do something." He wiggled his free hand, symbolizing the movement.

Liz began walking herself. "You know, there really is no such thing as spontaneous organization. Members communicate, sometimes tactically sometimes simply ideologically." Raymond followed and quickly evened out with her. "I know there is an utterly bizarre American ideal of 'one man making a difference,' but that's simply not how politics, not even sensational spectacles with a soupçon of politics, works."

Raymond said, "If you don't want to tell me, that's okay."

"What do you mean by that?"

"I presume you wouldn't be here with me if you didn't have some sort of plan."

"Perhaps my plan is to jump on the next bus."

Raymond said nothing. They hit 42nd Street and made a left, threading their way through the crowded streets, past Grand Central Station and toward the windy river.

"Ever been?" Liz asked. The slab tower of the United Nations rose on the horizon.

"No, actually."

"Why not?"

"I never get up to midtown. Never been to the Statue of Liberty either, or the top of the Empire State Building. All those famous places you heard about in Adelaide are for kids on field trips and tourists. Sometimes colleagues come into town and ask me what's a good place to eat in midtown and I have no idea. I counted seven TGIF's just walking up here."

"Hmph," Liz said.

"It's for tourists."

The pair walked with their cooler across the final street and onto the gardens and concrete rivers of the United Nations Plaza. Six blocks of flags fluttered on their identical poles, loud enough to Raymond's ears to make him wince. Acres spilled out before them, mostly empty of people save for the few police in their vehicles and at the security checkpoints. A pair of tourists snapped one another's photos by the twisted barrel of the handgun statue *Nonviolence*. A German Shepherd, tongue hanging and leash straining, a uniformed police officer stumbling behind, trotted up to the cooler.

"Got a bomb in there?" said the officer, a tall man with the skin of an African and just a trace of an accent. Then he laughed.

"Nope, dinner," said Liz. The dog sniffed at the cooler and, smelling something good, licked at it. We scuttled around the underside of the box to avoid the querulous nose, which jabbed and tapped as if trying to open the box. "Hungry dog, I guess. May I pet her, officer . . ." Liz peered at the badge. "Bakayoko?"

"'Fraid not, she's a working dog," Bakayoko said. "Would you put the cooler down and open it?" He pulled on the leash. "Come along, Sophie, let them be?"

"The dog smelled a bomb?" Raymond said.

"No, no. You'd know if she had. She goes wild, and there would be a gun to your head right now, and four or five to your back. But I'd like to see your dinner if you don't mind."

"Do you need a warrant, or reasonable cause?"

"This isn't America. You can have your picnic across the street at Ralph Bunche Park instead. That's America. All your civil rights are across the street, along with a park bench or two. Far more comfy there, eh?"

Raymond lowered his side of the cooler and told Liz, "Well go ahead." She just let go, letting the box slam and bounce against the concrete of the plaza. We were on the back, hanging on. Then Raymond opened the lid. Bakayoko nodded. "Another box, is it? Let's open this one as well."

"I'd rather not," said Raymond. "There's a wasps' nest in that box. I took it out of my mother's house on Long Island this morning. I had to take the early train out, get all outfitted with gloves and one of those hats with a fine mesh net all around, and a smoker too, to get it out. I've been dragging it around the city all day. I'm a professor at City College."

"And what about this dinner she told me about?"

Liz stepped forward, her mouth open to register a complaint about being spoken about rather than spoken to, but Raymond took her hand, "I'm an anthropologist," he said, then he waited for Bakayoko to fill the void. When the officer didn't take the bait, Raymond said, "I've had to put a lot of things in my mouth that I never thought I would. Termites. Whale blubber. Rats and scorpions. Goat penis. Pig brain, with ten-foot strands of nerves I twirled around a wooden fork like it was spaghetti. And I tell myself, whenever I'm in the field and working to make a connection with others, to experience their cultures and gain the trust of insiders, one simple thing. I tell myself that there are only twenty amino acids; these twenty acids form the basis for organic life on this planet. They've all been in my mouth already." He reached down and opened the wooden box in which the nest, fat and lumped like a cancerous heart, lay and with his finger teased out a smaller wasp. He held it up to Bakayoko, who doubled his grip on the Shepherd's leash; the dog wanted to explore the nest and the insects both.

"Dinner," he said, and put the wasp in his mouth, head first, his teeth decapitating it before it could awaken and sting. He dropped the stinger back into the cooler and closed the lid while he chewed three times and swallowed. In their box in the cooler the wasps began to stir.

It wasn't a crowd that had gathered as much as it was a ring of people just outside the situational space of Raymond and Liz's confrontation with the UN police officer. They were well dressed, coming from the United Nations itself—interpreters and accountants languid, with shoulders slumped in their suits; a few Latinos who stood close to one another and dressed in the industrial garments of cleaning staff; several more police officers, hands on their belts, walkie-talkies and batons just a twitch away.

"What we want to do is have dinner here," said Liz. "For the cause of solidarity. Under the flags, or on the grass by one of the statues. Beat your angry hornet into tasty protein. I'm the publicist. We'll be here nightly, like a vigil. We hope that people will start bringing their own foods, trading with one another, feeding one another. Did you know that in Haiti some people are reduced to eating dirt because the price of beans and other staples are so dear, thanks to peak oil? And that even the dirt is getting expensive now?" She nodded.

Bakayoko nodded back, mimicking what he saw. "I'm familiar with the consumption of insects and of course I read the papers, see every picket sign and desperate petitioner, hear the officials on their cell phones in a dozen languages, ma'am," he said. "Very little gets by me or Sophie." He reached down to pat the dog's flanks and to subtly examine the waistbands of Raymond and Sophie. No firearms, no wires, nothing clicking or ticking down or even blinking. "There is paperwork to be filled out, though, if you expect media to come here, or food to be served. Permissions to have, in hand, before you begin."

Raymond picked up his end of the cooler, with Liz quickly following. "If you can tell us where to go, we'd—"

"You can go," Bakayoko said, "home. To your phone book and Internet. It's nearly 8 p.m., there's nobody to take your calls now, no meetings to be had tonight." He pointed with his chin over Liz's shoulder and across the plaza and the First Avenue. "Or you can use Ralph Bunch Park, back in America, where anyone can eat whatever they like whenever they want." He laughed. "Ho ho, isn't that the truth then! And you bring us hornets to eat instead. How wonderful for you. How utterly brilliant. I'm sure you're a pair of those strange people performing all those foolish stunts for reasons of so-called politics. Playing Nintendo while Rome burns and takes the rest of the world with it. Thank you, but no. Take your vermin—pardon me, your amino acids—and come back some other day."

Raymond stood, his jaw stiff, not knowing what to do.

UN-BEE-LIEVABLE

Fugitive Ott Finds Parking Spot At
UN Plaza . . . The Hard Way!
David Schneider—Special to *New York Post*
June 23, 20__

Talk about your international incidents!

Fugitive Julia Ott Hernandez, who has evaded authorities since the shocking murder of real-estate developer Peter Neads Fishman nearly a year ago, made a run for the border last night by commandeering a tour bus and driving it into the United

Nations Plaza and through the visitors' entrance. Nobody was hurt in the escapade, but Ott Hernandez escaped again, though her estranged husband, CUNY professor Raymond Hernandez, also on the scene, was questioned and released.

Ott Hernandez, 32, boarded a Big Apple Tour Bus at approximately 6:30 p.m Wednesday. The bus, which was idling outside a McDonald's on 38th and Park, was unoccupied. The cherry-red double-decker weaved through late rush-hour traffic as it made its way to the United Nations, with Ott Hernandez using the bus's PA system to shout for right of way, but she did not attract police attention until getting within spitting distance of the United Nations. "That's when she gunned it," said UN police officer Randolph Bakayoko.

Ott Hernandez guided the speeding bus through a shrubbery and aimed at a small crowd of people that included both Raymond Hernandez and Bakayoko. They and about a dozen others ran for their lives as the double-decker swayed and rolled up the plaza, nearly slamming into some of the famed sculptures on the plaza. The bus took out two cement security pylons that had been put in place in front of the Visitor's Entrance after 9/11 and slammed through the glass doors.

"The husband started following her, dragging his picnic cooler and screaming her name, 'Julia! Julia!'" Bakayoko said. Moments before, Bakayoko said that he had been examining the cooler for contraband, and found that the professor was carrying a wasp's nest within. He radioed ahead to security within the UN complex. "I told them a bus was coming, and they told me, 'We know.'"

The rogue bus drove right through the marble-lined visitors' lobby at speeds of over twenty-five miles per hour, according to NYPD skid mark experts. "Our main concern was safety of the UN staff and employees, including physical plant staff," said UN docent Paul Sedia. "We cleared out everyone we could. We didn't know who the driver was until afterwards, when we reviewed the tape." The UN, which is outside U.S. jurisdiction, has its own police force and firefighters. "Our goal was site protection, not capturing a fugitive." The UN is cooperating with both the NYPD and FBI in attempting to locate Julia Ott Hernandez. She allegedly exited the bus, and assaulted Hernandez after he confronted her.

Hernandez made no comment as he left One Police Plaza this morning and has not been charged. According to one NYPD spokesperson, "Hernandez remains a person of interest in our investigations of Ott Hernandez but is not a suspect at this time. The wasp or hornet nest was not recovered. It is our understanding that the nest has some kind of cultural importance as regards Hernandez's work as an anthropologist."

Security surrounding the United Nations has been increased, and visitor tours are cancelled today and tomorrow.

RECORD OF TXT MSGS, HERMANN LIZ 6.22.__ VERIZON WIRELESS # 6468783435 MESSAGES RECEIVED

10:38AM - CALLING ALL CARS: Go find Queen Bee; John t/ Baptist just showed up. Go Jehovah on the doors in your hood.

11:02AM - YAY good idea

3:01PM - OMFG, WTG! UN U say?

4:20PM - keep it up; hey check the time!

```
o_0 =~~~
```

6:32PM – FUCK!!

7:48PM – SOS ABANDON SHIP

MESSAGES SENT
10:49AM – I'll knock on Johns door, OK?

2:15PM – QUEEN BEE IS HERE. Crazy claims :re totlzing nrrtiv. On way to UN, change history

4:18PM – CHECK IN OK

6:28PM – QB LFT BONNET

6:59PM – QB BACK – TERROR ATCK @ UN w BUS!!

7:14PM SHT HT FN. PLAN Z!

TRANSCRIPT OF INTERVIEW WITH RAYMOND HERNANDEZ, CONDUCTED BY DET. LOUIS ORANGE, HOMICIDE. 6/22/20__+1.
Q: Been a while since we last had you here, eh Doc?

A: Just about a year, I think.

Q: And how have you been?

A: Up and down.

Q: Up and down. That's something to say again. Up and down. Let me tell you how I've been, okay?

A: Please do.

Q: My son died in Iraq. Improvised explosive device.

A: I'm sorry to hear that.

Q: So was I. Right after whatsisname was found funneling all the money to Iraq too. You know, the feds believe that Julia secreted some money in a similar way from that web company she worked for? Isn't that an interesting coincidence. A lot of the movement people are against the war, you know? Some even want Iraq to win, to teach America a lesson, they say.

A: I can't keep track of the political positions of that movement.

Q: What can you keep track of, Doc? How about the whereabouts of your wife?

A: I had no contact with my wife until this afternoon. I'm sure you know that; I'm sure that the police keep an eye on me, tap my phone and email, maybe even put someone in my classes to audit me.

Q: So, when your wife made contact with you this afternoon, why didn't you call the police? Why did you follow her to the United Nations?

A: She followed me to the UN, I didn't follow her. I wanted to get her out in the open before contacting the police.

Q: So she could escape. Nice, harboring and abetting an escape. Thanks for letting me know—

A: No!

Q: No? What would you call it then? Your wife shows up after a year on the run, coming to ground right in front of you, and the first place you go is the United Nations so she can ram a bus through it!

A: No, I was in fear of my own life and the life of Liz, my new girl-friend, who happened to come by just as I was going to call the police. I wanted to get her out of the house—

Q: So you could go back to fucking your wife, the murderer and terrorist.

A: I wanted to get Liz out of the house, not Julia.

Q: So you hoped that Julia would stay with you.

A: I wanted to get to a public place. It's safer in public, isn't it?

Q: Not when people start hijacking buses and running them through buildings!

A: Nobody was hurt!

Q: Disappointed, I bet. Did she forget to strap dynamite to her chest, or was that going to be your job?

A: I think I'd like a lawyer now.

Q: I think you can get the fuck out of here now.

Gotham Apple Tours, LLC.
350 Fifth Avenue, Suite 1344
New York, New York 10118
(212)GOT-APPL
ridetoday@gothamappletours.com

June 23, 20__

Gus Petrakis,

Mr. Petrakis, this letter is to inform you that, effective immediately, you are terminated from your position as a bus driver, A1 for Gotham Apple Tours. This reason for this termination is due to a flagrant violation of the Gotham Apple Tours code of conduct, "driver shall always remain in vehicle when out of garage," and the Gotham Apple Tours employee handbook, which states, "Employees in the field may leave their vehicles for hygienic or medical reasons, **provided they radio ahead to headquarters for permission**" (emphasis added).

Please make yourself available at home on June 28,

20__ from the hours 11 AM – 4 PM, as a messenger
will be dispatched to retrieve the Gotham Apple
Tours uniform and other Gotham Apple Tours property. Please have the uniform cleaned and pressed.

Best,

GOTHAM APPLE TOURS, LLC

THE cooler was knocked over, the mutant nest splattered
against the floor like rotten fruit and the wasps flew in
every direction. Why did we let Julia and Raymond enter
the United Nations building and release *Hymenoepimescis
sp.* through their improvised fight? So we could destroy the
wasps once and for all, irradiated as they were by the radon
in Raymond's mother's basement. The United Nations is
our territory, a complex in which innumerable men and
women of indeterminate ethnicity can walk the halls with
impunity. Had we stopped the pair, perhaps we would
have lost track of the nest—unique as it was amongst
Hymenoepimescis sp. it may have attracted the attention
of scientists, many of whom are already familiar with the
wasp's targeting of *Plesiometa argyra*. We did not want this
form of attention.

Further, had Julia and Raymond been repelled,
either by us or by the human security forces of the United
Nations, the wasps may have remained free to consume us,
or to sting other human beings. Had Raymond retained
possession of the cache of *Hymenoepimescis sp.*, they may
have tried again and again. If not at the UN, then perhaps
at the White House or a meeting of one of the major
political parties. Finance capital could have been targeted,
or a convention of captains of industry. Better here, where
we rule the halls.

Julia's rush of the visitors' entrance gave us free
rein within the halls of the United Nations. Security was
tightened, but only to keep people out, not to track the

movements of men of indeterminate ethnicity who were already a part of the complex's daily life.

On the fourteenth floor of the Secretariat Tower, a Finnish envoy pinched a wasp with a tissue held between two fingers and quickly walked with it, arm out as if holding a lantern, to the men's restroom, where the wasp was flushed down a commode. On the way back to his desk, he spotted another insect and with his elbow smeared it against the Vermont marble slab wall of the hallway, but it was not *Hymenoepimescis sp.*

In the Dag Hammarskjöld Library, an American library assistant wheeled a cart of VHS videotapes being collected to transfer to BD-R over two of the insects. She stopped over their bodies and ground her heel into the mess, just to be sure. Another American vacuumed up a wasp and, sad to say, the *Plesiometa argyra* the wasp had cornered and mounted, in the media gallery of the Security Council chambers.

In the gift shop, on a Thursday afternoon when the store was quite crowded, we spotted a wasp and quickly moved within our cashier of indeterminate ethnicity to destroy it. We had cornered it and held a world atlas to our chest to crush it against a wall, but the wasp managed to sting us on the hand. We dropped the book and clamped the hand under an armpit. Our legs were unraveling within our slacks as we ran for the restroom and we barely made it to the stall to kick off our left shoe and flush the disincorporating webbing down the commode before I FELT LIKE SPAGHETTI ON A FORK TWIRLING AND FLYING TILES SINK LITTLE BOY SCREAMS RUN TOWHEAD BOWLCUT SKITTER SCATTER RUNRUNRUN FLOOOOOOOSH

In the General Assembly, a representative from the Ivory Coast rose from his chair and slammed his fists and hands repeatedly against the table in front of him, bellowing all the while about French imperialism. When he managed to crush the wasp that had been attracted to the spiders within his form, he sat back down. We were thankful he did not disincorporate due to a lucky sting, but after our previous encounter we adapted and were quite methodical in our fist-slamming—the first three shook the table sufficiently to upset our enemy, the fourth damaged her stinger and the final flat palm smashed her utterly against the slick pressed wood of the tabletop.

It took over a week, but we killed them all, every one of them.

20

THOUGH social animals, individual *Homo sapiens sapiens* are often much like *Hymenoepimescis sp.*: predatory, individualistic, and cooperative only to the extent a spontaneous order emerges from simultaneous anomistic decisions. That was Plan Z. It was declared as a possibility and yet left undefined. Spoken of in a few isolated but widely heard exchanges between partisans, but its content was occulted. Plan Z could be called upon by anyone in the movement at any time, but was never fully described, in order to keep it from being used by the marginal figures who may have found a sense of community and personal importance within Sans Nom. Movement propagandist Snarly Temple referred to this concept as "Mutually Assured Confusion."

Plan Z was sufficiently opaque a concept that a number of people took it to mean that the movement was to be disbanded. Some people attempted to turn themselves in. Jorrie Torres, whose post-Fishman campaign involved moving to Brattleboro, Vermont, and standing in the Harmony Parking Lot in the middle of town while wearing a pair of paper butterfly wings and holding in one fist a roll of quarters and in the other hand a sign reading **FREE HUGS AND/OR A PUNCH IN THE FUCKING FACE**, reported to the local police department for her punishment.

"Dearie," said the bored looking police officer at the front desk, as he folded his copy of *The Reformer* in his hands, "even in these latter days of the law, where tyranny and sadism seem to have filled to overflowing the scales of blind justice, there ain't no criminal statutes about being *tedious*. Scram!"

On the West Coast, Plan Z was more directed, even explicitly political after a fashion. A flash mob in San Francisco formed on Fisherman's Wharf and swarmed over the pleasure boats. Sails were unfurled, some engines hotwired—other ships were actually owned by members of the mob who boarded their own crafts with keys jingling—and a flotilla launched themselves into the bay and toward Alcatraz Island.

The drive toward the prison island was chaotic. Some ships were handled by fairly accomplished sailors, while others were captained by enthusiastic tyros. A few ships bumped into one another, creating obstacles for other ships to slam into. A half-dozen small sailboats found themselves winding in ever-widening circles, their bows oriented toward Alcatraz but then drifting away, only to orient back toward the island again several minutes of waving arms and shouting later. Still, nearly forty pleasure craft had managed to chart and follow a course toward the island. Banners were rolled down the sides of several the larger ships, with messages reading **I CAN HAZ FREE DREW NOW** and **INVISIBLE JUSTICE** flapping in the breeze.

Police boats and a barge used by the FBI to handle the massive number of parcels mailed to Drew Schnell from admirers and movement members moved to intercept the flotilla. A police loudspeaker demanded that the ships disperse and return to their port. Flares were fired in response; they streaked just over the bows of the police boats. Three military helicopters took off from the prison's courtyard and dipped low over the waves, turning the warm waters to a frothy chop, and sending some of the lighter and less competently handled sailboats tilting on their sides.

"Turn back!" The sound was nearly swamped out by the chaos of the waves, the shouts between boats in the flotilla, and the hollow warp of the digital amplification. "You are in violation of federal law. We will fire upon ships that do not turn back!" Those power boats owned by their drivers began turning back, and in a hurry, engines roaring. The water boiled with wakes streaking back to Fisherman's Wharf, but this further upset many of the sailboats. A few sailors had megaphones of their own and shouted back, "Don't shoot! We can't drive this thing!" and "Help!" The barge was brought into position and police boats managed to corral many of the small craft that couldn't or wouldn't turn back. Only three ships, all under sail and all manned by one or two white males, washed up against the island. Divers were quickly deployed to pluck the Sans Nommers from the waves; they were then brought to the prison and arrested.

And the plan worked. For one of the correctional officers—a deep-cover agent with the rather obvious pseudonym of Doug Graves—was a member of the movement. While the flotilla swarmed outside in the Bay, he entered the cell of Drew Schnell, quickly gave the prisoner a haircut, and gave him an orange jumpsuit with another prisoner ID number. He then moved Schnell to a broom closet. When the rescued invaders were handcuffed together in a hallway to be dried out, Graves added Schnell to the line and changed the headcount to reflect the additional prisoner. Graves, exercising a little CO discretion, then put the whole line in a large holding cell and waited for the shift to change. The new crew, which came onto the island for work at 8 p.m., had not seen the new prisoners, and all the records had been updated by Graves to match the new reality. Schnell, Graves, and the others were transported by police boat to San Francisco County to await bail.

Once in SF, Graves dropped his badge in a sewer and paid for a Chinatown bus ticket to Los Angeles with cash.

Schnell, when asked to identify himself before the police at morning headcount in the county lockup, did so honestly: "I'm Drew Schnell," he said. "I was snuck in here by a CO as part of an attempt to free me. This is all part of the plan." The local COs, working from reports from the divers who picked up the movement members on the rocks of The Rock, figured that Schnell was just a local movement wiseass who broke into prison, and sent him on his way. Schnell spent several hours in the San Francisco Mission District begging for change, in order to buy a wig that matched his old haircut from a discount store. Once so outfitted, he easily found someone willing to drive him across country, back to New York.

At the end of that week, the real Plan Z was instituted. The World Wide Web went away.

★   ★   ★

It wasn't all that hard. Globally, there are only a handful of registrars and root servers, the machines that tell web browsers that 216.109.112.135 is Yahoo.com. It was a simple denial of service attack, but instead of attacking Yahoo.com or Whitehouse.gov, the movement attacked the registrars and root servers. The hackers who received Liz's Plan Z message turned to their keyboards and enslaved servers—it was easy, most of the conspirators actually worked for server farms in the first place. They used the machines to make tens of thousands of http: requests to root servers at the very foundation of Internet traffic. Then there were the viruses, sending the same program out to tens of thousands, then hundreds of thousands of other machines. Embedded in email—you've received these, haven't you?—the viruses did not attack hard drivers or make nuisances of themselves to the end user who received them. Common subject headings included **I JUST WANT YOUR HALF** and **SANS NOM NOM NOM** and **PLEASE HELP US DESTROY THE INTERNET TODAY!!**—enough members of the movement downloaded them, as did the usual dupes and marks, to enslave their machines as well. Whatever resources the user wasn't actually using, the virus was, to send http: requests to the roots, and to replicate and distribute itself via email client address books. After twenty minutes, one thousand major servers were pinging the roots and registrars ten thousand times a minute. After an hour, forty thousand servers and half a million PCs were hammering the servers with a billion requests a minute.

The servers quickly failed. It was nothing an end user would notice at all, except that every URL in one's bookmark file, and any other location one tried, began to fail. Not CNN.com, not NYTimes.com, not Facebook, and not even the annoying websites that usually pop up when someone makes a typographical error. The language of the web was derailed, as if Google and Yahoo and Twitter and Blogspot meant nothing at all. It wasn't even a domino effect—imagine a fragile and beautiful collection of dominations, arranged to collapse in a wondrous splay across the length of a football field, then the field itself erupts into fissures and collapses.

A few people were able to remain connected—at first those Plan Z cell members had a virtual monopoly on the entire environment. They'd carefully memorized or written down the IP addresses, those lists of numbers that the root servers translated into easy-to-remember words, and could thus continue communicating with one another, and post and upload what they liked on the sites for which they had accounts. Of course, there were many technicians who also knew the IP addresses of their own home sites and other pages that were their responsibilities, but they were mostly very busy, these poor men and women. They were all on the phone, handling dozens of calls at once.

Then the landlines and cell phone servers were overwhelmed. This wasn't even Plan Z. One might call it Plan Z+1. What letter is there on the edge of the English language? The Greek *Xi* with his bubbling hiss between tongue and palate? A Laotian tone? A !Kung glottal click? Millions of users gave up in frustration, sure that the 'net would be back soon enough, but millions more immediately called tech support, their personal geek friends or relations, or random numbers they found in user manuals or CD-ROMs. Cable companies. Baby Bells. ISPs. Their bosses. Their underlings. The local brick-and-mortar version of the store whose online phantasm faded away so abruptly. That football field of dominos, now a steaming hole? Let's say that forty thousand tons of concrete and bleachers fell into the chasm as well.

Surely you remember those three nervous weeks before the web was recovered. Sure, some things still worked. Corporate intranets. Some landlines in overbuilt (or underpopulated) areas, though often just occasionally and only thanks to thousands of employees mobilized as temporary telephone operators—"May I have the number you are trying to reach please?" was no longer the wind-up of a half-remembered and obsolete joke of an even older sepia-toned time; it was the catchphrase of the year.

ATMs and the banking system were generally all right, though one wouldn't know from the long resigned lines that twisted around blocks and blocks. The line, that was the new *on*line, the new World Wide Web of flesh and resentment that tried to form in place of fiber optics and plasma screens. The virtual marketplace crumbled, but a new infrastructure began to take its place. It didn't so much "spring up" as it congealed, slowly, around the legacy technologies of the daily newspaper, sold again on street corners in thrice-daily editions, in extended banking hours when checks could once again be drawn by hand and traded for scrip, in the new "slug mobs" of desperate jobseekers who stalked the streets with banners reading **BANDWIDTH OR BUST** and blocked the street traffic to regain that sense of mastery once provided by a virtual world only a mouseclick away.

Davan ate a handful of sleeping pills. Alysse saved his life by leaning him against the walls in the corner of their apartment and slamming her fists into his stomach until he vomited up the pills in a soup of old food and new blood. She broke four of his ribs and nearly ruptured a kidney. She visited him in the hospital when she could—she was only allowed to every third day as patients now lined the halls two deep—and left him by the end of the week. She hitch-hiked back to Ohio to live with her parents, who had a large garden and three German Shepherds. "Call it Plan Z+2" she wrote to Davan in a crooked, girlish script. The postcard took three weeks to arrive.

Wallace, that old police officer from Trenton, hardly noticed what was wrong till the next morning. The rabbit ears on his old TV still worked, and he found a UHF channel broadcasting emergency information direct from the FCC. He reported for work and stayed on duty for nine days straight, catching what he called his "da Vinci" naps— fifteen minutes, eight times a day. The young Turks at the precinct took his lead. He remembered life as it had been; he changed typewriter ribbon, dug out the old walkie-talkies with portable handcranks, and in a junk shop in Camden found enough vacuum tubes to get the old dispatch radio sets running. He liked to ride shotgun—let the snotnose drive—and he liked holding his shotgun in his hands with the windows rolled down so everyone could see that they'd better behave on the streets like it was 1959. And in Trenton, thanks in no small part to Wallace, they did.

Liz herself wasn't quite sure what Plan Z was, even as she pulled the trigger on the endeavor. She'd thought of it, she told friends over drinks in the first of four candlelit nights in the liquor store whose security gates she they had jimmied open and then closed behind again for privacy, as a giant reset button. "Like in a video game. Something that would erase what had come before." She took a long pull on the jug of wine and smiled a purple smile. "I was right too, eh?" Liz's friends, mostly just yellow eyes in the dark, tittered and drank their mid-shelf vodkas and improvised appletinis. Liz knew she'd be fine. She was Australian, they were mostly American.

It only took three or four hours for most of them to drink themselves into various stupors—some were silent, others snored like engines. Then she picked herself up out of the small puddle of urine she had produced and on wobbly but thick legs let herself out and locked the rest of her movement cell in the store indefinitely. There were enough nuts and chips to keep them alive, and when they were found and freed it was only en route to an arrest. Nobody else in the world knew that it was Liz that had called down Plan Z, and nobody was going to believe a quintet of drunks with radioactive orange Cheetos Flamin' Hot with Limon Crunchy Snacks powder caking their lips. Louis Orange, doing street duty like all the other police officers, found them and—worried that they were a cult who might be attracted to the word on his badge—maced them all before arresting them.

★ ★ ★

Gus Petrakis was rehired by Gotham Apple Tours, as the company had quickly developed a new business model and needed their buses on the streets twenty-four hours a day. Gus spent the hours between midnight and eight a.m. driving National Guardsmen and bags of money across the five boroughs of New York City and occasionally onto Long Island and into New Jersey. When they thought nobody was watching, Petrakis and the male guardsmen would climb to the roof desk of the bus and urinate off the sides. The lone female in the troop, who had met Julia months before, often pantomimed raising her weapon and firing through the ceiling of the bus.

A NEW WORLD IN OUR HEARTS? AN ANARCHIST RESPONSE TO "PLAN Z"
by Free Africa Bong – *NINTH ESTATE BROADSHEETS*

The last month has seen an unparalleled revision of the state of human affairs. Ever since Z-Day, when the Internet "went down", many millions of people have been getting down with mutual aid and a world without the technological crutches of electric cash, online "relationships" (which are nothing of the sort), and individualism. When the proverbial shit hit the fan, we were all given the same choice: adapt or die. For righteous anarchists, this was easy. We'd already adapted, creating our own penumbra of infoshops, skill shares, collective homes, and real human interactions based on human needs, the middle classes and privileged sets were left scrambling. Of course, now that most sites are back online and everything is returning to **BUSINESS** as usual, we have a chance to do something big.

Yeah, the so-called "movement" was really a bunch of middle-class assholes, but those middle-class assholes did what we spent the last seventy-five years talking about: they dealt a body blow to capitalism. And what do you know? From the power vacuum emerged all sorts of cool new nonhierarchical social formations to deal with the new 'Net-free environment. So yeah, thanks middle-class assholes! We owe you a solid. Maybe slightly longer ropes when it's time to make use of the lampposts.

And hey, wasn't it great NOT to be a slave to the sell phone and the Crackberry for a few weeks? To get MAIL in the mail instead of credit card come-ons and coupons for things you'd never use even if KKKorporate AmeriKKKa paid you? To walk by a bank and laugh at all the people who THOUGHT they had money when all the really ever owned were promises in convenient-to-carry electron form?

But now the 'Net is coming back! Hell, the big sites were back online after the first five days, and when people rushed back to continue their "virtual" (you know, as opposed to "actual") lives, the bourgie dumbshits just crashed them again with their sheeple stampede to their old wretched lives. We were able to distribute more *NINTH ESTATE* than ever before. And people said the Mimeograph Machine was dead!

So here's what we want you to do:

If you didn't take an axe to your computer on Z-Day out of pure frustration, do it today out of PURE JOY!

Keep it on the streets! You don't HAVE to go back to your job even though your "workstation" is waiting for you, nor do you have to stay home and somehow "connected" via your "playstation." Don't abandon your new comrades, comrade. Keep the hustle and flow flowin'!

Make copies of this and other issues of **_NINTH ESTATE_** you've been collecting over the past three weeks! We have a circulation of nearly 100 now, and any set of eyes we can get our hands on helps! We need to get busy on the sheets!

Send us money: the **_NINTH ESTATE_** collective isn't getting any VC funding or government grants! Draw us up a check. If you see an **NE** comrade, bring him a tasty vegan sandwich (we <3 fennel) or a new pair of pants. We need one another, now more than ever!

★   ★   ★

BRIAN Bernstein, also known as "Free Africa Bong," the former owner of Williamsburgist.com, and the founder and only member of the *Ninth Estate* Collective, was found beaten to death outside the Common Ground coffeehouse of Athens, Georgia, with several copies of the above broadsheet crumpled into balls and shoved down his throat. Police investigators determined that the material was pushed into his mouth while he was still alive.

21

I T took seven hours for Raymond to get out to his mother's house on Long Island on the evening of Z-Day. The cab he was in, and for which he had paid an even thousand dollars, actually ran out of gas in the traffic on the Northern State Parkway. The cabbie had to pour the emergency reserve in the trunk into the tank, and then learned his lesson. He turned off the ignition, and then turned it on again only when cars began to slowly crawl down the highway. After idling for a five minutes, he'd turn it off.

"No A/C, sorry," he told Raymond.

Raymond opened one eye and muttered, "That's all right. Nothing to be done. Hell, for most people on the planet, getting from Manhattan to Suffolk County in ninety minutes would be considered magic. Maybe we deserve this big kick in the ass."

"Whatever," said the cabbie. "I still gotta find a place to sleep on the island after I drop you off, if all this shit keeps up."

"It'll keep up."

"Yeah, I know," the cabbie said. "It's worth it for a G. Hope wherever you're going is worth it to you."

"My mother's house. She's probably freaking out, trying to call, kicking the TV if it doesn't work. She's a delicate person. I know she's worried sick and probably also somehow blaming me for not picking up the phone, as if I could." Raymond sighed and that sigh turned into a yawn, and he didn't bother covering his mouth because the cabbie was only making eye contact via the rear-view mirror. "So I have to drag my butt—and yours, and sorry about that—out

to the North Shore so she can yell at me for the world
falling apart. But at least she'll know I'm alive, so she'll be
happy." Raymond turned his gaze to the strip of woods
beyond the highway. "It's also not smart to be in the city
right now, I think."

The cabbie said nothing and the two waited for
hours. It was 2 a.m. by the time Raymond entered his
mother's home, where he had been just a few days before.
He switched on the lights in the kitchen and looked in the
fridge. The sounds of static fuzzled down the steps to the
upper floor, where Raymond's mother kept her bedroom.
Raymond ate some meatballs in sauce from a pot, with his
fingers, then sucked his fingers clean and closed the door.
He stretched out on the couch and fell asleep immediately,
his right hand tucked into his pants.

★   ★   ★

RAYMOND woke to the smell of burning bacon. He shot
up and off the couch, and ran from the living room to the
kitchen to grab the pan off the burner. "Mama!" he called
out. He dumped the bacon and the black grease into the
sink, and peered out the window into the yard over the sink.
Then he grabbed a few paper towels and wiped the basin of
the sink clean, so his mother wouldn't know he had poured
grease down the drain instead of collecting it separately in
the old coffee can used for that purpose.

"Mom!" he tried again. And he walked upstairs. He
looked into her bedroom. The bed was made and the TV
still on, playing static as the cable was out. He checked his
old bedroom, a shrine to his high school years laminated
in dust and kitsch. The L. L. Cool J poster was especially
disconcerting, the yellowing science fiction paperbacks
a bit less so, but he had no time to rifle through them or
pack a bag for his eventual trip back home. He checked
the upstairs bathroom, which was empty, and the tub itself,
which was dry, so mother hadn't been taking a shower

recently. He ran down the steps and checked the mud room, and then went down into the basement. It was piled with boxes and cracked furniture, and cool as it had been a few days prior. The path he had kicked through to get to that pile of blankets and find the mutant *Hymenoepimescis sp.* nest was still in place, except for one patch of floor on which a small wicker basket full of old socks had rolled.

Raymond went back upstairs and into the small yard with its hip-high chain-link fence. His mother wasn't in the back by her tomato plants or in the front getting the mail. He reached for his cell phone and checked for messages but he received a No Service notice. He went back inside and picked up the receiver of the wall phone in his mother's kitchen, and there was a dial tone, but the few calls he tried to make—to his own voicemail number, to Liz, to Mama's friend Irma who lived around the corner—all failed. Raymond walked out the house and headed toward Irma's, but walked back after half a block and sat down on the couch where he had slept. The living room TV wasn't receiving a cable or broadcast signal either, but there were DVDs, and he put on *Like Water for Chocolate*, which his mother had cued up. Raymond drifted off to sleep again and we had him. Now all we needed to do was find Julia and reinsert her in the Simulacrum as well.

22

THERE were three worlds now. The world as you knew it, the emergent world of tyranny and cooperation that had emerged in the wake of Z-Day, and the Simulacrum. Julia had more places to hide. The security apparatus on which we often exploited was in disrepair and human behavior had become somewhat less predictable after Z-Day. Yes, there were explosions of rage and frustration and indeed there were instant communities formed in the crucible of disaster, but who found themselves pulled toward what was essentially arbitrary. Like the weather, the anthroposphere has an infinite number of variables and predictive analysis is thus inexact in the best of times. To create and make indispensable a communication network that size and scope of the World Wide Web over the course of half a generation, and then to dispense with that network, albeit temporarily and partially, was an unparalleled event in modernity. *Hymenoepimescis sp.* and its role in the evolution of your species seemed nearly superfluous.

With three worlds to hide in, Julia was difficult to find. She knew of the Simulacrum now, and how to find her way back into it. In the chaotic world of Z-Day, she could be just one more flailing quartet of limbs hurtling down a human-choked street. And in the world of blogs and e-commerce, Julia might still be there, one of those few with lists of IP addresses and the power of access. There she might stand out, but on the Internet anonymity is still a possibility, especially when one only passively consumes. We had a thought—Julia may be somewhere out there, in an interstitial space between worlds—spying on us, plotting her revenge.

What would Julia do? Would she make friends, which she is very good at, and charm her way onto a steamer headed toward the Panama Canal, and there seek out the *Hymenoepimescis sp.*? Perhaps she would even infect herself a second time, to bring still more larvae back into the U.S. with ease. Was there a doctor among Sans Nom that could extract them? An entomologist who dabbled in etymology on the side? Julia's behavior would not necessarily be further altered, as the wasp in the wild wouldn't have been irradiated and mutated as were those she encountered in that Long Island basement. Julia would always know of us though, and would be fuming with rage and anger, as humans nearly always do when they encounter another form of intelligence.

Or was Julia active on the Internet, such as it existed during those weeks? When the root servers and registrars went back online, would the world be greeted to a YouTube video explaining it all, or a Facebook application designed to turn a genocide against us into a fun game to be played amongst friends?

Perhaps Julia was in the Simulacrum again, playing the role we assigned for her as best she could, given the eruptions of Z-Day. Her flight from the United Nations was the last we'd seen of her, though on the edges of our own World Wide Webs we felt vibrations, a presence.

★　★　★

"THIS is not a poem," Julia said into the microphone in the Der Rathskeller. It was dark and smoky. So much anxiety over the past few months—antismoking laws were lifted in many municipalities. The room was a warm one, almost too warm. A couple of men, both wearing thick plastic eyeglasses, had just walked in. Indeed, we followed them. Their lenses steamed up instantly, and they sat half-blinded.

"This is the truth," Julia said. "This is the story of the motherfucking world." She raised her left hand and the droning of the theremin on the podium at her waist increased in volume then, with a twist of Julia's right hand, altered pitch from a low thrum to a wild whine.

"Vladimir Lenin," she declared, enunciating every syllable with an angry precision, "played the theremin!" She looked older now, her hair was streaked with silver and matted into ropy dreadlocks. She was gaunt from the stresses of hiding, of irregular diet and of a different couch each night, her face faceted where bone met the backside of flesh. Her sundress hung off her like a drapery. "The audacious dictator, an enthusiastic student of electronic music." The theremin squealed, then Julia lowered both her hands, nearly touching the silvery box, and the few men and women at this performance felt the decline into low sonic rumbling in their thickest bones.

"Why!" Julia said. She pulled her hands away from the antennae on either side of the instrument. Now conversational she said, "Whether you are a Leninist, and even on a college campus these days there likely aren't all that many, or not, it's a pretty bizarre little factoid, isn't it? Was he the leader of a great working-class movement or a ruthless dictator? Either way, whatever your opinions, he took time out of his day and during a civil war that threatened not only the new socialist society but Russian civilization itself. The war was not only against the future but the past as well." Another gesture, another warbling wail.

"The theremin is a unique instrument. Look ma, no hands!" Julia whipped her hands behind her back and the sound vanished except for the atonal buzz of the power supply, and the rhubarbhubbub of the patrons. Then she slowly brought her hands back around, her fingers swaying at her waist and then resting just over the machine. The sound came to life again, animated like the yawn of waking. "There is another difference as well. With a theremin you play the rests as well as the notes." She angled her hands slightly, twitched her fingers, then turned her wrists—the symbol of the movement—and the tones warbled and burbled in response.

"Lenin believed that rest was retreat. He thought he saw the strings behind the system and wanted to do away with them. He thought electricity, and his political party, would combine to create a new world, a third world where the sphere of political will met the sphere of materiality, and with a spark"—her right hand's index finger stabbed the air and summed up a quick waaaAAAAOOOOooo from the aether—"utopia!"

The man in front of us waved for the waitress and with a bark ordered the chicken tortilla soup. His eyeglasses had defogged; his eyes were a dead blue. He felt our stare and turned to look past us, to show that he did not care.

"If you are paying with a debit card tonight," Julia said, "You will receive fifty thousand dollars, from me, tomorrow. It will be credited to your account." She waved her hands over the instrument again, creating a hollow-sounding moan. It sounded like sex. "This money is not tax-free. Questions will be asked of you by your bank, your government." There was a change in pitch.

"If you are paying with a credit card tonight, you will be granted a fifty thousand dollar credit line, not attached to your current card. The material will come in the mail to the address associated with your account within seven business days."

"What if we pay cash?" someone shouted from the side of the room. He wore a bushy beard and straggly curls in his hair. A beret as well, too small for his head.

"You get nothing!" Julia screamed. "You are fucked, boy! You get that? Your little arbitrary decision to throw a few greasy fives onto the table means you are out of luck. You fetishize the fucking *real*, monkey." A hand up raised the volume of the theremin's rattling wash of white noise. Julia shouted over it, sounding as though she were at sea. "There is an unseen world out there. Cash is old magic, it's the dumb wizardry of signs and tokens. Go get a pen and write your own ass a check." Then she lifted both hands high above her outside and outside the field generated by the theremin's antennae. The atonal buzzing began again, sounding like a refrigerator that was just about to break down for the last time.

"The world is an electronic thing. Lenin was half-right: electricity and political will led to something new, but it wasn't the worker's paradise of tractors and singing babushkas. It led to a world that is ready for a revelation. The Big Invisible just up and went and took five trillion dollars with it last summer. Now you know, now you all know how arbitrary the intersection between your meat-rix bodies and your matrix jobs is, eh? There was something out there, as subtle as plumbing and intimate as speech. Ook ook, Caveman Jones. And then you didn't get to have it a month. Did the world go poof and transform back into 1987? No. We played the rests as well as the notes, and we did the best we could. And we learned something too, didn't we?"

Julia turned purposefully away from the corner of the room at which the man who had heckled sat and addressed the rest of us. "The invisible is important. It's new magic—in the old days we might say we had our grandfather's axe: our father replaced the handle. We replaced the head. Now we say we have our grandfather's axe and point to a digital photo of a pile of chopped wood. You dig me?"

She ran her hands over the space in front of her, making the theremin waowaowaowao. "Do you? Do you dig me with two g's? Well here's another bit of performance poetry for you to dig!" she said.

"We are not the only ones here!" Waowaowaowao went the invisible air. Even in our man, our mass of appendages pulling and yanking on the strands of webbing that mimics musculature—we play the rests as well as the notes—tingled from the fullness of the sound in the tiny rathskeller.

"There is another amongst us." Vrrrmmmmmmzzzzzzzzaaaaoo.

"They twist and turn and fight and flex and shift and suggest. They exist within the spaces. Spiders, I tell you. A secret breed. A distributed brain covering the planet in an organic, pulsating, venomous world wide web."

"Preach it!" It was the man who had paid in cash again. We turned as one, not just us but the human patrons as well, to glare at him. Julia ignored him this time. "We live in their web," she said, "and they sometimes live in webs with the shape and mien of men."

Perhaps we should thank *Hymenoepimescis sp.* If there was a less efficient way to try to jumpstart the understanding of *Homo sapiens sapiens* with regard to our existence, we could not have programmed Julia to embrace it instead of this. For a moment we contemplated letting her go free, to see how she might evolve with the parasites inside her, and with her experiences in the Simulacrum still functional enough so that she was largely unrecognizable despite the continued notoriety of her murder of Fishman and the movement it sparked. She was unique in all the world, in all three worlds, and in her own fashion she was expressing this difference, manifesting it, in front of this small crowd. There would be much to learn from observing her life cycle. Then we thought the better of it. Who knows what damage she might be able to cause in the future? The pawn who could once again be queened. Every conflagration starts with but a spark under the right conditions. Julia was still a spark, begging for air and fuel and finding little of either on that stuffy Wisconsin evening.

The lights dimmed, save for a pale blue spotlight on Julia's narrow face. It floated in the dark. The theremin opened with a deep *mmmmvvrrraaaaaow* tremolo into higher pitches as Julia's unseen hands swayed. "There is another intelligence on this earth. It is not above us, but it is beyond us. It watched us with a million unblinking eyes brachiate through the trees, trundle over the ground on heels and knuckles, pick up the stick and write the word. It's been waiting for us for a long long time. Can you feel them, waiting for you?" The final light was brought down and we were all in the dark.

"They wait."

The music ended as well, even the humming of the idle theremin wound down. For a long moment all was still except for the rushing of blood, and for us only, the gliding of Julia's bare feet off the stage, and some shuffling immediately before us, a pair of breaths sharp and shallow. We waited till the lights were on to rise from our seat. The men who had been directly in front of us were already gone.

They were easy enough to find, along with Julia, in the alley behind the venue. The two men had cornered her and the theremin she held against her chest like a shield, and one had a firearm in his hand. She was by a windowless white van, its backdoors open. Mud was splattered across the license plate rather too artfully. We interrupted them by walking into what the men considered their personal space. The man without the gun—his sweater was tight against his muscled body, and he was older despite attempting the casual wardrobe of a younger person—reached into his front pocket for his wallet, and then let it drop open to show identification. "FBI. This isn't your business, sir. Step back for your own safety." The other agent raised his gun to Julia's head and held it with both hands to show how much our presence did not distract his attention from the woman he hoped to capture.

We stepped forward and said, "Don't." The agent spun on his heel and put a bullet into the chest of the man we rode. Several of us fell from the hole and onto the dusty floor of the alley, where we fanned out to get into a better position. We were surprised and a bit impressed that the agent responded to us simply by lifting his arm a bit and shooting our head to pieces. Yet more of us fell from our man of indeterminate ethnicity—the brainpan was full—and rolled down the shoulders and chest, some of us clinging to our clothing and trying to climb back to our station. We lurched ahead despite the reduction in personnel and grabbed at the agent. Julia raised the theremin above her head and brained the other man, who was just now withdrawing his own firearm, and then bashed in the back of the head of the man with whom we were grappling. She turned and then ran back into the café, confident we'd be loath to follow. Other men of indeterminate ethnicity were nearby, but not so close as to grab Julia. Some of us went after her, to keep her under observation while the rest guided our man to the sewer drain at the far end of the alley and disincorporated the shambling vehicle of the man so we would not be discovered.

In the café, Julia was accosted by three of the patrons, all of whom had either a Blackberry or a laptop with them. One had jokingly checked his bank account balance and did indeed find the fifty thousand dollars, which led the others to check their accounts as well. "Thanks!" one of them, a man who was dressed much like the FBI agents, but organically so, said, but he was slapped lightly on the arm by a woman with long hair severely parted down the middle.

"Are you nuts?" she said. "This is a crime!"

"It's not a crime to give someone money," said the other man, a thin boyish one in a T-shirt that hung around him like a sail.

"We have to file with the federal government when we deposit more than ten grand in our accounts, and explain where we got it from. Plus, this could be money laundering," the woman explained. "Crazy things like this don't happen for no reason, and never for a good reason." She turned back to Julia. "Listen, I liked your performance. It was provocative, an entertainment. But you're squicking me hardcore here. I don't want to be a prop in your scene."

"Well," Julia said, "the thing of it is—" and then she dropped the theremin on the woman's foot while scooting backwards herself. The woman screamed and clutched at her leg. The men exploded, shouting, "You crazy fucking bitch!" and one of them swung at Julia, but was too slow and tripped over the theremin itself. Julia ran back to the van, slammed the doors shut behind her and *on* several of us, then peeled out of the alley at high speed.

Julia drove off the highway at the first exit she could find, into a sparsely populated farming area. She cut the headlights and drove up to a small farmhouse. Luckily for her, the place she chose had a pickup truck in the driveway, and it was unlocked. The keys were even inside. "Ah, the Midwest," she said to herself as she transported her few bags to the new car. She quickly changed her clothes and then withdrew from her purse a small palmtop computer with a GPS application. A unique random number generation subroutine chose a destination, and then altered it every few minutes (also at seemingly random intervals). Though the technique was limited by the long stretches of highways and relatively few exits that cut across Wisconsin and its neighboring states, Julia did manage to get herself to a remarkably remote area by the time she stopped to pull into a rest stop under the red candied dawn sun—there wasn't a man of indeterminate ethnicity for a hundred miles around, and there were few enough of us in the pickup truck that we could not spin a fresh one large enough to subdue Julia or drive the car. We did start to spin a someone, however.

Julia snored in the front seat till the dew evaporated. Then there was a knock on the glass of the driver's side door—a coincidence that actually worked to our benefit. The thin fist knocked again, almost belligerent, and Julia awoke and groggily rolled down the window after finding the handle with which to do so.

Alysse held up a picture of Julia and asked Julia, "Pardon me. I'm one of many people on a worldwide hunt for Julia Ott Hernandez. We're knocking on doors, and any sort of portal, really, all over the planet and I was wondering if. Oh."

In the baby of indeterminate ethnicity we built in the cab of the truck, we initiated a hysterical wailing. Neither Julia nor Alysse could ignore it. It was a cry that called out to their very chromosomes. Julia jumped in her seat and tried to swing the door open, but Alysse caught most of the force with a wiry strength and managed to shut the door again on Julia's leg. She reached in and grabbed the keys from the ignition, and got Julia's elbow in her teeth in exchange. Alysse spun away from the car, bleeding from the mouth, and whirled around, throwing the keys into the wooded area right on the lip of the rest stop. We howled for attention, and people in the two other cars—one a recreational vehicle and the other a small hatchback—began to stir. Alysse went low and tried to tackle Julia as she limped out of the car, but Julia pivoted her hips and spun on her good heel. Alysse slid past her and nearly banged her head on the side of the stolen pickup as she skidded to a stop.

The man in the hatchback stuck his head out the sunroof and waved a cell phone. "I'm calling 911!" he announced. "I'm calling 911!" Then he rested his elbows on the roof and watched Alysse and Julia square off. Alysse's baggy light blue button-up shirt was spotted with blood from her bleeding mouth. Julia was game and a head taller, but limping badly and her left pant leg was soaked and sticking to the flesh.

"My gawd, why are you fighting?" shouted a heavyset women from the RV as she approached the truck. She popped open the door to the cargo area and fetched the baby we'd spun from it. "You two whores should be on your knees right now, begging the Lord for forgiveness!" Alysse stopped and looked chagrined, but danced out of the way when Julia lurched toward her. We needed to introduce more uncertainty into the situation, so one of us crawled from the mouth of our baby and bit the woman carrying us in the arm. She yowled and fell to her knees, clutching us tightly. Then the man in the hatchback finally flipped open his cell phone and called the police.

"Grab that baby," Julia said to Alysse. "We're out of here!" Experiencing a moment of latah, Alysse obeyed instantly and snatched us away from the heavy woman, who was beginning to go into shock from our venom. Alysse rushed to the pickup and slid into the passenger seat. Julia limped past her. "Get out, moron!" she said to Alysse. "You threw the keys away." Then Julia marched to the RV and hoisted herself up into it. Alysse followed immediately. The doors slammed, the engine roared to life and Julia backed it out of the spot.

"Don't run over that lady," Alysse said.

Something groaned from the back of the RV.

"Go take off your top and have sex with whoever is back there," said Julia. "It's probably the husband."

"Uhm, what about this baby?"

"I've never seen that baby before in my life," Julia said matter-of-factly. "Does it look like me? Would you think someone would leave a baby in a pickup for me to steal and it would just start crying at the very dramatic moment it did? Think about it, girl, there are forces beyond compre-hension manipulating us at every turn."

"True," Alysse said. "But I'm beyond that sort of thing."

Julia snorted. "For example, didn't you leave your car behind just now? Haven't you been swept up into an entirely different scenario than what you anticipated?

"Oh no," said Alysse. "I walked to the rest stop. I'd been walking all morning. I wasn't just looking you as part of"—Alysse twisted her wrist—"I was also walking. I've been walking all month and blogging about it as part of a campaign to raise awareness for oil-addiction and alterna-tive forms of transportation."

"I didn't realize that feet were an alternative form of transportation," Julia said. Alysse had no response to that. "Do I really have to have sex with that guy back there?" He groaned again and nearly fell from his couch.

"Whatever, just keep him busy. What state is this, by the way? I've been driving all night at insane and illegal speeds."

"Ohio."

"Of course. Which way is Hamilton!, Ohio?"

"Hamilton!" Alysse shouted with a smile, and she pointed down the highway. Then she got up, put us down on a bench, from which we nearly slid to the floor of the RV, and began to unbutton her blouse.

23

HAMILTON! Ohio is a name one must practically shout, as the signage on the roads leading into the city all have an exclamation point at the end of the name. Alysse and Julia took turns shouting "Hamilton!" as they drove toward the city, and when they shouted so too did the man Alysse had tied to the fold-out couch with strips of her blouse, except that he was also gagged by the cups of Alysse's bra. Alysse had selected an oversized flannel shirt from the tiny closet space and wore that instead.

"What gender is the baby?" Alysse asked. She turned her head to look back at us.

"Dunno, didn't check. I imagine it's probably flat in the genitalia," Julia said. She told Alysse what she had pieced together, about *Plesiometa argyra* and the men of indeterminate ethnicity. Then she shouted "Hamilton!" as she saw a highway sign (though it lacked the exclamation point the city's own signs have) and Alysse joined in and the man in the back of the RV growled through his bra-gag.

"Say," Alysse said, turning back again, "is your name Hamilton?" Hamilton nodded, his eyes large but cracked with red veins. His face was purplish-drunk but shifting toward hangover-gray. "Wow, that is a bizarre coincidence!"

Julia jerked the steering wheel hard nearly sending us off the chair on which we lay. She pulled the RV to a quick stop on the shoulder of the road and clicked on the hazard lights. "Forty-five seconds," she told Alysse. "We have to keep moving." She turned the radio on and quickly found a tinny AM station on which a preacher was going on about Revelations, then cranked it up.

"Hello, Hamilton," Julia said, leaning over her captive. "If you act up, I'm going to stomp on that baby's head." She pointed to us. And then spiders will pour out of it." Hamilton flexed against the strips of shirt binding him. "Looks like she was a Girl Scout, eh, with such knot-tying ability. Anyway, Hamilton, this is not some kind of *Thelma and Louise* thing, really." She drew herself up and put a finger to her chin, considering. "I mean, I did shoot a man, but his gender was incidental. Incidental to my shooting him, that is. Certainly, he benefited from being male throughout his business career and was able to interact with a variety of old boy's networks, the Mafia, City Hall, and all those other male-dominated spaces thanks to his gender and his roly-poly mien."

"Ten seconds!" said Alysse from the cab of the RV.

"Anyway, what I'm trying to say, Hamilton, is that I am a bad motor scooter, so don't try to be a hero. I eat murder and poop ideology. I learned to play the theremin in three days. If you fight, you lose. So just chill. I'll take off your bra so you can join in the conversation." Julia undid the gag. Hamilton stretched his jaw twice and licked his lips and said, "You are a crazy woman. You left my wife back there. The police are surely after you. Why not just turn yourself in?"

"Into what?" Julia said, and then she went back to the cab and got behind the wheel.

We restructured our throat a bit and spoke to Hamilton in the squeaky baby voice provided by our chosen anatomy. "Hello. Do not worry. All will be well soon enough."

Hamilton fainted. The RV revved to life again and in a few minutes we were in Hamilton! Ohio, squeezing down the narrow lanes of High Street.

"I'd ask what the plan is, " Alysse said, "but you'd just change it after telling me, right?"

"Right," said Julia.

"This is so strange. If Davan—he was my boyfriend, until recently—tried to pull something like that off, I'd be very cross with him." Alysse turned to Julia. "Do you remember me? I'm the one who told you about Fishman. With Davan."

"Why do you think I punched you in the mouth?" Julia said. "Where do you park an RV around here?"

"You don't. Well, not outside of RV parks. I don't think there are any in the town proper. Maybe over by Miami?"

"This is good. Go fetch Hamilton."

"Why?"

"We need him to carry the baby." Julia stopped the vehicle in the middle of High Street. Traffic was light, but built up behind the RV instantly. Only Midwestern manners kept the honking and screaming from starting as Julia and Alysse stepped out of the car, followed by Hamilton, with us in his arms.

"Run!" said Julia, and we all did. There isn't much to run to in Hamilton! as the residences tend to be squat and surrounded by the sort of cheap chain link that transforms human communities into innumerable fiefdoms of barely coherent nuclear families. There is only a brief main drag of low-rise buildings and the omnipresent chain stores: 7-11, McDonald's, Starbucks, JiffyLube, et cetera, and the occasional stirring building of stone and failed hopes. Banks, local ones that had seen better days, and old remnants of the economic reach of Chicago, long since withered on the vines of the highway system. Outside of the !, there was hardly any life in Hamilton at all. This is because Hamilton is a node of the Simulacrum.

"Hamilton," we whispered into the bosom of the man named Hamilton, "turn right immediately!" Hamilton obeyed, his legs twisting before his mind even fully understood that he was being addressed, the psychological phenomenon of latah at work once again. "Another, right! Go!" we squeaked in our infant's voice. He found himself on a side street. "Up those steps!" Onto a loading dock. "Through the door!" And we were everywhere. A giant web, great balloons of spun silk teeming with life. Hamilton nearly dropped us, but it wouldn't have mattered. A man of indeterminate ethnicity walked through the curtains of webbing and silk, and held open his hands.

"It's an odd thing," we said, "when coincidence works in our favor. Hamilton, thank you." We took the baby and held it. "Every one of us is precious, especially in these tough times. There are so few of us, we cannot cover the world sufficiently well to help everyone through their hard lives. But there are so many of us it is increasingly difficult to keep our existence secret from you."

"Well," said Hamilton, his voice weak and ghostly. "I can keep a secret. I can." He turned away from our man, but couldn't help but see us scuttling along strands of webbing, spinning, and knitting, no matter where he turned his gaze. "Oh, Lord," he said. "I apologize. We meant a collective you. Your species. Don't worry, we'll not harm you. Indeed, even now we are working to reunite you with your wife. We've also sprung your RV down from the impound lot." We put the baby down in a hammock lattice of web and those of us animating it crawled out, leaving behind a crumpled husk. Hamilton started backwards, his feet demanding egress, and walked into another wall of webbing. He shrieked, flailed, and then doubled over to vomit.

"Oh my," we said. "That wasn't quite right for you either, was it? We don't normally entertain people. Sorry."

"Oh God, oh God, I need to wake up. I'm still in the trailer, still tied up. That crazy woman with the little boobs and her maniac friend. That's so much better than this." He turned to us. "Listen, you can trust me. It's not like anyone would believe me, even if I told them what was going on here. Even if I led them to this very spot. Uh, not that I know where I even am. Not that I would bring people here, or come back myself with a can of gasoline and a torch." He sank to his knees, resting on the vomit. "You're going to kill me, aren't you?"

"Oh no," we said, very concerned. We moved the face of our man to make us look concerned as well. We were concerned. "We don't want you to get the wrong idea. We

are quite peaceful. We do not kill other intelligent beings."
He stared at us, eyes wide and skin nearly as pale as those
eyes. "We are sure you qualify," we said, as jokes lighten
mood. He did chuckle a bit. "We would like to arrange your
life so that this no longer upsets you, yes?"

"Yes," he said, though if he had said "No" we would
have simply assumed that he was negating the idea of his
life continuing to be upset by us. And we introduced him,
and his wife who was in a nearby hospital waiting in the ER
for treatment for our bite, into the Simulacrum. It took the
form of his RV, filled with high-octane fuel and prepared
with new car smell, and a slightly less interesting itinerary
for the remainder of his trip.

We've said before that coincidence tends to work
against us, and indeed it did. Julia knew, or guessed at least,
that Hamilton! was an element of the Simulacrum. Her
random paths around the Midwest were designed to keep
her within a day's drive of the city, to let her watch our
comings and goings, our reactions to her sorties and sallies,
just as we have watched hers. While the U.S. is a pheno-
typically diverse area, it is true enough that in much of the
great stretch of flat and farm, and in the shivering cities that
depended historically on river rather than ocean traffic, men
of indeterminate ethnicity tend to stand out. Simply put,
she had lured us out into the open.

"And Hamilton!" she said, turning that last word into
a shout though she was out of breath from running, "c'mon.
The exclamation point gives it away. Geographers rejected
it, the bang doesn't appear on the maps, but it still stands
out in the town itself."

"Why would the spiders need to signal to themselves?" Alysse asked. They were both catching their breath
between two Dumpsters that reeked of chicken fat and cut
grass behind a KFC, where a few of us were sitting in the
sun, waiting for flies.

Julia shook her head. "It's not a signal, it's a tell. They
cannot help themselves. They're not quite human. Nobody

on Earth thinks having an exclamation point at the end of a town, especially a Podunk little burg like this one, is a good idea. That's why there aren't any others, right?" Julia threw up her hand, and ran her finger through the thick, knotted dreadlocks of her hair. "It's like this," she said. "Can you understand your cats and what they want, all the time? You had them since they were kittens, right?"

"How did you know I have cats?"

"I can tell from your haircut and tone of voice. It's a demographic inevitability."

"Uh . . . okay," Alysse said. "And yeah, I found one as a rescue and she was already pregnant. Then she had kittens. And then over the years they got old and died and whatnot, and I only had Stymie left."

"And did you?"

"Know what Stymie wanted all the time? No, of course not."

"Same with them and us. They're not bad. They're would-be jailers, but like overprotective mothers. And they're terrified. They whipped up a fake little life for me, and fake little lives for—God, who knows?—millions of people. They just can't tell what we want. They spend their time thinking, 'Hmm, maybe people want to be happy. Maybe we should play with them, or give them Royal Crown Cola or uncomplicated orgasms, or just leave them alone or pay them close attention.' There just isn't a lot of communication between the two species," Julia says. "Unlike cats, though, they're frightened of us, not imperious towards us."

"Frightened of what?"

"The Orkin man, I presume. It's not like we haven't wiped out species before. We do it every day, by accident. And one that might be a threat, that is older than us and maybe smarter than us?"

"Yeah. I'm feeling a little genocidal myself." Alysse leaned heavily against the Dumpster and wiped her forehead with the thick flannel of her shirt. "It's so strange, even thinking of there being someone else out there, with us.

Even maniacs and dictators, hunter-gatherers, millionaires, child molesters. We all have something in common. We're human, you know. We shit, we fuck or want to fuck, we smell things. It feels like we're all in this together, somehow. Maybe we should tell the world."

"They are the world, or at least a big hunk of it," Julia said. "We should keep moving. Police station. Nobody pays attention to white women in police stations."

"Sweet. I know where one is," said Alysse. "I got drunk here once with my college boyfriend and keyed some SUVs. They kept us for seven hours and tried to make us eat bologna sandwiches, even though we told them four times that we were vegetarian."

"Fight the power."

We followed them for the several blocks to the police station and indeed, Julia had become an insightful observer of the human condition. The officer at the front desk did not look up at the pair of women, despite Julia's ragged appearance and the splotch of blood on one knee. Alysse's fat lip didn't get much attention either. Traffic came and went. There were sandwiches delivered and dissected—"Fucking pickles," the desk officer declared, followed by "Fucking coffee"—and phone calls handled. The scanner was on, and calls crackled across the vestibule. Alysse closely examined the Most Wanted lists hanging on the wall. Julia had her ear on the scanner, tensing when the RV was mentioned and declared impounded. She didn't jump right up and rush out the door though, as that would have been information that even a semi-somnambulant desk officer would have recalled at a later date. Instead she counted to herself, subvocalizing, lips shifting subtly, to nine hundred. Then she waved Alysse outside.

"Got a cell?" she asked Julia on the steps.

"Sure."

"Good. I was worried you'd have a paper cup and a single string as part of a movement to raise awareness about alternative forms of communication. Call information to find out where the impound lot is."

Alysse did, and the address was on the far side of town. "How about a cab?" Julia said. "Do you have cash?"

"Well, I promised myself not to take a car, but I guess I blew that already with the ride this morning. I mean, Julia . . ." Alysse ran ahead three steps and then turned to face Julia. "I think, I have to tell you, this is just great. It's amazing. The changes we've made. We shut down the Internet! I realized what a jerk Davan was. People are doing things all over the world, and it's all thanks to you. It's an honor to be here with you. I feel like Samwise to your Frodo. This is a real adventure."

"Samwise?" asked Julia.

"He was the heavyset hobbit. Played by Sean Astin? Hello?"

"Let's keep moving. I'll pretend by heavyset guy from a movie you mean Don Corleone. That way we'll both be happy." Alysse dialed information again and got a taxi dispatched to the corner on which they were standing.

The drive to the impound lot was silent, though the cabbie kept glancing at the pair of banged-up women, nearly ready to say something.

"How much cash do you have?" Julia asked Alysse, *sotto voce*.

"A couple hundred in each shoe."

"Good," she said. Then to the cabbie, Julia said. "Listen, we're waiting for an RV to come rolling out. We'll give you a hundred bucks to follow it to wherever it's going. It won't go out of town, at least I don't think so."

The cabbie leaned over the seat, his elbow resting on it. "And why should I do that? There's only one reason why anyone ever wants a taxi driver to tail another car?"

"Really? What's the reason?"

"They want to follow the driver to the home of his mistress, or to the local bordello." He shrugged. "Two locations, but it's the same reason, you know?"

"Well, do you think it's okay to have affairs?" asked Alysse.

"I think it's good business not to get involved in domestic disputes."

"Two hundred," said Julia.

"Done," said the cabbie.

Alysse turned to Julia, her mouth open. Julia reached up and closed it. The cabbie subvocalized the word "dykes."

Hamilton, accompanied by a few men of indeterminate ethnicity, arrived at the impound lot, and claimed the RV. We allowed Julia to follow us back to the large warehouse on Millville Avenue, on which our local headquarters hummed and spun with life, and from which we engineered the Simulacrum town.

24

Alysse had her cell phone out. "Should I text
people?" she asked.

"To what end?"

"I dunno. What's the plan? Maybe we need people to
help us brainstorm?" Alysse said. "A critical mass."

"That's spider talk," Julia said. Then she smiled.
"Text who you like. I'm going in. I have no idea what will
happen, or what I'll see. Maybe I just miss the lover they
assigned me."

"A lover?"

"One of them," Julia said, pointing with her chin
toward the warehouse. "Well, dozens of them probably, like
that baby. They changed me, you know. They didn't change
be back to the way I was either. I was a stung by a wasp that
had altered my personality. The spiders are just parasites of a
different sort, and more awful for it because they think they
know what we want, while the usual run of parasites just use
their hosts as channels for nutrients and whatnot."

Alysse texted a number she hadn't tried in weeks:
Davan's. **HEY**, she typed, **M WELL U?** "Is that why you don't
have a plan? The changes?"

"Who can say?" Julia said.

Alysse put a hand on Julia's shoulder. "Well, we can!
Let's figure it out."

"How do you propose we do that?"

"We can figure out what parts of you are essential,"—
she glanced up at Julia's hair—"like not the dreads, and
which are contrived. It's like psychotherapy, except we have
to figure out a way to do it right now." She pursed her lips.

"Hmm." Then, "Okay, free association. Um, should we do this right here?"

Julia shrugged. "Good a place as any, eh? If I'm right and this town is just a reality-prison, it hardly matters where in the cell we stand."

"Fish," Alysse said.

"Man," said Julia.

"See, most people would say water," Alysse said. "Oh, I shouldn't kibitz."

"No, you shouldn't. Give me more."

"Dread."

"Lock."

"Maybe I shouldn't look at you when I do this," Alysse said, turning her head.

"Wear."

"House?" said Julia. "Or did you mean wear like in wearing clothes?"

"You're not supposed to kibitz either!" She hmphed. "Love."

"Hate," said Julia.

"Spiders."

"Squish."

"Wasp."

"Sting."

"Point," said Alysse.

"Bang," said Julia.

"Peace."

"Shattered, or did you mean piece as in piec*es*?"

Alysse turned back to Julia. "Would your answer have changed?"

"No, not really," Julia said. "Listen, this is a waste of time."

"Not waste, Julia, spend. This is us spending time." Then she pointed to a VW microvan that had just turned the corner and was cruising down the street. "I got us a ride. Let's just get out of here. There's nothing in that warehouse for you but another rewriting of your personality. Let's go fuck some more shit up."

Julia grabbed Alysse's wrist and started dragging her to the gate of the warehouse, which we had left closed but unlocked. Alysse pulled back and kicked at Julia, but the older woman was stronger, sinewy, and determined. Drew Schnell emerged from the van and rushed to Alysse, grabbing her around the waist and pulling her back. Alysse grabbed a thick sausage of Julia's hair, but Julia twisted her neck and shrieked. She then quickly turned and slammed into Alysse and Drew both—her push met their pull and the trio fell to the floor. Julia scrambled to her feet and Alysse followed, but Drew simply untied his Doc Martens boot while still sitting on the ground, slipped it off his right foot, swung it around his head by the laces and hurled it at Julia. It bounced off her back and knocked her off-balance.

"Jesus!" she said. "What the fuck was that?" She glared at Drew, bent over nearly double, her left hand reaching for her lower back.

"I got another one," Drew said as he dove for his other boot. Julia snatched up the boot that had just hit her and lobbed it, underhand, at Drew's face. Alysse rushed at Julia again, but was swept to the floor and had her arm twisted behind her back for the trouble. Drew's other boot sailed over Julia's head and through a window into our warehouse.

"Uch," said Alysse through gritted teeth. "Now you've fucking done it. Let me go, God!"

"Nice throw, asshole!" Julia shouted at Drew, who was finally picking himself up. She twisted Alysse's arm even further, into a full hammerlock. "Any closer, and I'll break her arm."

Drew walked calmly toward Julia. "Go ahead. It'll heal." Alysse squirmed, but Julia grabbed a fistful of her hair as well and said to Drew, "Will her fucking face heal too if I smash it against the concrete?"

"Probably," Drew said, not breaking his too-slow stride.

"Why don't you want me in that warehouse?"

"Maybe we do, but we're now just trying to find out how much you want to be in that warehouse," said Drew.

"Ever get the feeling that everyone else in the world has free will, but you are a slave to forces beyond your control?" Alysse asked, as best she could with her nose to the warehouse parking lot. "Or, how about vice-versa?"

"Well, which is it?" said Julia, grinding Alysse's cheek against the ground. Alysse squeaked defiantly.

"Are you kidding?" asked Drew. "We were hoping you'd know." He was over her now, though with his pot belly and scruffy peach-fuzz hair he did not impose much of a visual threat. Julia loosened her grip on Alysse, who lifted herself up on one elbow and brushed gravel from the pocks of her face.

"We don't even agree with one another. I think you are free, Julia."

"And I think the spiders are calling the tune."

"How do you know about the spiders?"

"My lawyer's one of them. After I escaped from prison and helped launch Z-Day, they found me again and brought me here. We're a lot alike, you and I," said Drew.

"And how did you end up in Hamilton?" Julia asked Alysse, her *Hamilton* lacking the crucial burst of enthusiasm at the end.

"Well, uh . . . I was actually born here," she said, sheepish. "This is where I grew up. It's a real town, it's not just some lame Potemkin Village. It's just that nobody really wants to be *from* Hamilton. I mean, would you?"

"I certainly fucking wouldn't," said Drew. Julia let Alysse go entirely and stood up.

"Hamilton," Alysse said, walking off a cramp and dusting off her thick shirt, "used to be notorious. They wouldn't let army guys come here because High Street was full of speakeasies and whorehouses." She waved her arms around. "This was a bedroom community for the Chicago mob! Not that I'm in favor of organized crime or anything, but, you know, that's pretty cool."

"Maybe when you were a kid, but the town has since been under the lathe of lockstep," said Drew.

"There weren't speakeasies when she was a kid, Drew," Julia said.

"So you agree with her?"

"No."

Alysse frowned. "I had a real life here."

"One that you left for Brooklyn, which you wanted to save from gentrification," Julia said.

"True enough, but that doesn't make my experiences any less real, or any more of some kind of biochemical cliché. And speaking of . . ." Alysse gestured toward Drew and studiously looked him up and down. "Who are you supposed to be? The Comic Book Guy from *The Simpsons*? Even this ridiculous philosophical conundrum is nerdy. Clichés are everywhere."

"So you're still a snotty high school bitch, just like you were before the spiders came and took over, huh?" Drew said.

"All right, this is entertaining," said Julia, "but I'm going in. It doesn't matter whether I am going in due to my free will or because I've been programmed to. What matters is that I am going."

"I'm coming with you," said Drew. "This is like the *Twilight Zone*." Then he made a sound remarkably like that of a theremin.

"I'm coming too. Of my own free will," said Alysse. "Let's see the strings that control the system."

We opened the doors for them.

25

I F we were to describe our own philosophical position vis-à-vis the thorny question of free will, we'd identify as compatibilist. It all seems rather self-evident to us. Our webs can only stretch so far; there are limits—cognitive, chemical, temporal—to our collectivity. We're all finite beings in an infinite universe, and indeed, *Hymenoepimescis sp.* more or less guarantees that some of our own actions cannot be predicted, even by ourselves.

We consider the issue a solved problem, really. Our species is rather less argumentative than yours.

Drew entered first, his face a twist of fleshy emotions. Julia was right behind him, her arm touching his back. Alysse dawdled behind and stayed in the well of the entrance for several seconds. "Jesus," she said. A man of indeterminate ethnicity, the same who had just dealt with Hamilton and put him back in his RV, greeted them all.

"Busy day today," we said with a smile. We tried to keep our skittering along the criss-crossing beams and spheres of our webs to a minimum, as too much activity upsets people, but we were all eager for a look.

"Why are you doing this?" asked Drew. "Revealing yourselves to us."

"We're here for the genocide," said Alysse, suddenly pushing her way up front.

We took the opportunity to practice raising our eyebrows.

"They're fresh out, I bet," said Julia.

"We mean no harm."

"Take us to your leader," Drew said, then he laughed a miserable little heheheh.

"Take us to yours!" we said.

"Davan's not here," said Alysse.

"Davan's the *leader*?" Drew said. Alysse stared at him with a look of poisoned disgust.

Julia walked up to us, close and intimate, her breath on her face. "Sorry," she muttered. "They sort of followed me."

"We know," we said. "It's all right." Julia slipped her arms around us, her hands sliding between the crooks of our elbows, and she squeezed hard. We responded, wishing we had more limbs.

"What's going on?" said Alysse. She had her cell phone out again, her thumb poised. We weren't sure ourselves.

"What is going on is what should go on when intelligence meets intelligence," Julia said. "Some effort at something. These little guys"—she continued, her eyes up at the canopy of webbing that hung from the catwalks and the girders of the warehouse—"they try. They fail, they ruin lives, but they try."

"Heh," said Drew. "You ruined a few lives without trying."

"And we tried to limit that," we said, "with our intervention into Julia's life."

"That ruined a few lives too," said Drew.

"So did moving too late," we said.

"This is fucking ridiculous. Does everybody get to wreak some havoc but me?" Alysse said. "I want to be down with some motherfucking crime for once!" She darted to the wall and before we could stop her yanked on the fire alarm. The bells clangalangaclangalanged and the sprinklers began to fire. Webs fell like sheets from the ceilings and the walls. We fell hard but landed lightly, and some of us swirled down the drains or splashed about in the storming puddles born in cracks and pits on the concrete floors. Our hair got in the eyes of our man of indeterminate ethnicity. Drew threw his hands over his head and tried to duck the rain, but could not. A thick sheet of webbing fell on him, and he tore at it, then swiped his palms at his scalp and ran outside, itching and twitching at the spiders on him.

Alysse whooped and grabbed the axe hanging
on the wall by the alarm switch and starting swinging,
trying to cut floss as though it were wood. We, with
Julia—her arms still around us—shuffled out of the way.
Alysse ran into the billowing sails of webs and the rain of
falling spiders.

"Are her dreams of mass murder finally coming true?"
Julia asked us. Her dreadlocks had unraveled a tiny bit, and
dark water spilled from her face. Our feet squished in the
puddles in our shoes.

"Not really. She may as well be tearing up old train
schedules as far as we're concerned. We're mostly all here
and we don't have the same attachment to single little bits
of motivation and locomotion that you all do."

Julia rested her head against our chest. She pressed
hard with the side of her face, her ear, likely eager for
the rush of breath and the thump of a heart. Our men of
indeterminate ethnicity don't have those sensations on offer,
we're afraid. "You care about me, don't you? Love me?" Julia
must have hoped for a deep sound in the chest when she
said that second to last word, but there was nothing in our
man to hear. For a moment, we feared that we would be
revealed, so we said what we had to.

"I love you, Julia, very much. More than anything."

"Why?" He voice cracked.

"If we didn't, there would have been much more
bloodshed. There still could be."

"Bloodshed." Julia said, with a snicker. "Little bits of
motivation and locomotion suddenly spasming and coming
to a stop." She knew.

Alysse ran by behind us, splashing wildly, her axe
swaddled in webbing, a howl of glee on her lips.

"It adds up," we said. "And it delays the day we can all
meet as equals. If *Hymenoepimescis sp.* oviposits in a human
rather than in one of us, we benefit in the short term. But on
those rare occasions in which the wasp has been mutated,
changed by random bursts of radiation . . ."

"You lose," Julia said. The sprinklers tchtchtched to a stop finally, out of water.

"Everyone loses. *Homo sapiens sapiens* shattered the atom. There's more radiation now. The ozone layer has been chewed away by the gnashing of industry. We could explain it to you all, at once, so you'd understand, but you may not listen. It's so hard to know things, Julia. So hard to see the failings, and the flailings, of others—"

"The failings, you mean."

"No, the flailings. As in a web, each jerk and yank leading to further enmeshment. But we have to look, we cannot turn away. It's—"

Julia was a head shorter than us, and our man's musculature was contrived. She didn't notice till we spiders started falling on our head that we'd stopped speaking because Alysse had run by and lopped off our head with her axe. She gasped, then jerked away. The body, headless except for elements of the jaw, stayed upright and rocked slightly as we evacuated it. Julia scooped up a handful of us and mouthed empty words, then gently put us on the floor and waited as we scuttled away before stepping up to Alysse.

"Having fun?" Julia asked.

Alysse's breath was ragged, her arms lip, the hatchet blade's corner nearly on the floor.

"He wasn't real. Obviously," said Alysse. "So it doesn't matter. That's the whole point, right? None of this shit is real. That's what the whole thing with Fishman was about?"

"Oh, he was real."

"Until he wasn't anymore. And the money Drew sent to Iraq wasn't real, it was just a matter of mutual agreement. And the whole Internet going down showed just how much time everyone spends being unreal—playing at being hot, or at being a dragon, or being smart or having money," Alysse said. "Picking and choosing, that's the power you had."

"It's not power. It was chemicals. Wasp larvae, looking at me to design a world more amenable to them."

"How?"

Julia raised her arms. "More spiders out in the open, I guess, for the wasps to infect? More international trade, or at least multinational thrashing about by rich assholes, so they can spread. Maybe it was just an evolutionary mistake. The spiders just spin a different sort of web when they're infected. None of this was supposed to happen."

"What *was* supposed to happen?" said Alysse. She raised the axe again, huffing as she did.

"I don't know, I think we should just all back away from this," said Julia. "There is a whole other world, half a world, anyway. You know—towns like Hamilton!"—she stopped to chuckle because the exclamation point was still funny to her—"that they built or maybe just found. I've been there. It's not bad."

"Heh," said Alysse. "I just want your half. Is it real?"

"As real as anything else."

Alysse threw the axe away and winced when it clattered as it bounced off the floor twice before settling. "I want things to mean things. I want things to be real. I want to be an agent, you know, a social agent." She smiled. "A *secret* social agent. Doing stuff that matters."

Julia made a point of stepping between Alysse and the axe. "Well, you can tell the world if you want, about the spiders and the wasps. How much more important and widespread these two little species are. I'm done. I'm going to go see Raymond."

"Where is he?"

"The Simulacrum."

"Do you want to go, or are you being pushed to go," Alysse asked, "*pulled* to go."

"All of the above," Julia said. "They can't hold me there, even if they can get me there. You know?"

"Okay. I'm taking some of these spiders and webbing, and then I'm going to the newspaper. Not the local one, a real one."

"Well, good luck with that," said Julia, and she left the warehouse.

Deadly Dance of Wasps and Spiders May Lead To Rewriting of History Books, Lone Scientist Says
By Donna Barringer, *New York Times*
October 30, 20__

Scientists have been enamored with the *Hymenoepimescis sp.* since 2000, when it was discovered that the wasp was capable of changing the behavior of the *Plesiometa argyra* spider via the implantation of its eggs into the arachnid. The wasp sting temporarily paralyzes the spider and allows for the laying of eggs, which in turn feeds on the spider's fluid as they grow into larvae. The spider is "reprogrammed" by the larvae to create a unique cocoon-like web that can bear the weight of the wasps after they pupate and consume their host.

"There are many parasites that have developed the ability to neuromodulate," writes Elizabeth Slankard of the Miami University of Ohio's Department of Chemistry and Biochemistry in a letter to the editor of the latest issue of *American Scientist*, "and humans are not beyond having their own behavior modulated by parasites." Dr. Slankard believes that *Hymenoepimecis sp.* and similar species may be responsible for much of the evolution of human societies.

"The wasp's neuromodulation of the spider is very finely directed toward certain ends. It is interesting that the indigenous cultures of the areas of Latin America where the wasp is found never developed wheel technology, though they were advanced in other ways." Civilizations related to the Olmec had made many discoveries in astronomy, built irrigation canals, and had developed an impressive pharmacopeia based on native plants, but had never invented the wheel or established regular trade relationships with neighboring tribes.

"The wasp retarded the growth of these civilizations, to keep competition from invasive species to a minimum, and to keep their own habitat from expanding past the habitat of their prey species, *Plesiometa argyra.*" Lankard, in her letter, notes the architectural similarities between the unique cocoon-shaped web created by these spiders under the direction of the wasp, and the homes built by these tribes.

Researchers have long speculated as to the extent to which cultural evolution is shaped by exogenous forces. "Did hallucinogenic fungi in rye bread cause the hysteria that sparked the Salem Witch Trials? Did Saint John eat the wrong mushroom before writing the book of Revelations?" Dr. Jonathan K. Wolf, professor of history at New York University asks. "Was Caligula's horse really smarter than the average senator once the amount of retardation caused by drinking water from lead pipes is taken into account? These are rhetorical questions. Ultimately, the answer doesn't really matter. Philosophers like to talk about a universe without free will, but when you get down to the nitty-gritty, hard determinism renders the study of history incoherent. I don't think naturalists are going to find many social scientists willing to make themselves redundant for the sake of competing research programs."

That, according to Dr. Lankard, is the problem. "Research into neuromodulation represents a paradigm shift, and it takes massive amounts of evidence to shift a paradigm. And massive amounts of evidence," she said during a telephone interview, "requires massive amounts of funding." To that end, she has taken the unusual step of appealing directly to the public, asking for donations on a website called WebOfHumanHistory.org.

"I've been threatened with having my tenure revoked, I cannot get my work published," Dr. Lankard says. "But this is important research and it must go forward." Lankard says she became interested in neuromodulators after the so-called Z-Day event when over 95 percent of the World Wide Web was rendered inaccessible by hackers. "It just struck me, a real 'eureka' moment, about how tenuous everything is and how those webs of connection between us are so fragile. Pluck one string, and everything follows."

Myrin Sollazzo, chair of the department in which Dr. Lankard works at Miami University, would not comment on claims of tenure revocation, saying that "human resources matters are necessarily confidential," but did express satisfaction with Lankard's teaching of introductory biology and ecology courses.

About Lankard's fundraising website, Dr Sollazzo simply said, "Intriguing concept. I'm reminded of that bumper sticker, 'One day we'll have all the money we need for education, and the Air Force will have to hold bake sales to buy fighter jets.'"

26

RAYMOND found his mother's body behind a shrub on the border between her property and that of her neighbor Irma. The police and medics assured him that Lynn Hernandez had died of natural causes, and the death certificate declared that the cause of death was virulent and undetected lung cancer, likely due to extended exposure to radon. After the interference from Z-Day subsided and Raymond was able to make regular contact with his colleagues, he requested a sabbatical to write his book on penis panic and latah. It was granted easily enough, as the economy was in such poor shape that CUNY was cutting lines and retrenching entire departments. Luckily, Raymond's mother's home was paid off and there were enough gold and silver knick-knacks on the mantelpieces and in the hutches to pay for several years' property tax and home heating oil.

Raymond didn't write his book. He wrote to Liz and asked her to join him on Long Island. It took two weeks and a follow-up email for Liz to answer. She wrote:

From: Lizziepsygirl@comcast.net
To: hernanr@ccny.cuny.edu
Re: Please Come

Raymond,
Jesus Christ, I am about three seconds away from coming down there to "be with you" only so long to slap you across the face. Who on Earth asks someone to shack up with him, as a lover, via email?! And then doesn't even bother making a

```
follow-up call? Z-Day's over. If you wanted me,
you could have contacted me. It's perfectly ob-
vious that you are still mooning over your ex,
and that, my friend Raymond, is actually the
least of your problems. I am sorry your mother
passed, and that you are experiencing various
issues related to your career, but I cannot help
you. I am not a substitute for everything else
that is missing in your life, and you are not a
lab rat with a gambling problem who lives in a
Skinner Box so you are beyond my professional
expertise, though honestly I believe I would
like to electrify the floor under your feet.

Do yourself a favor and forget about me. I've
already forgotten about you. There is no need
for further communication between us.

yrs.
L
```

Of all the words in that message, the one Raymond took most seriously was "yrs.," and so Raymond wrote Liz back, asking if she would at least meet him at his apartment and help pack his things. Liz agreed that she could do that, yes, but only if an exterminator was called to spray down the place and all its contents beforehand, which Raymond's landlord did.

The packing didn't take long. Liz stormed through the four rooms, jamming everyone of Julia's possessions and everything that she suspected might be Julia's into one of the several large contractor's refuse bags she had brought with her.

"Are you separating them out for the Goodwill, and some for eBay, and some for—"

"The incinerator," Liz said. "All consigned to the flames, not the consignment shop. This is the best way to help you pack." She leaned over the bureau whose top she was clearing into the bag and found us. "Oh no," she said, snatching one of our appendages between her forefinger and thumb, "looks like one of the little buggers managed to hold his breath!" She waved us in front of Raymond's face. He flattened against the wall, surely due to Liz's thick and aggressive stance. "Well, the exterminator was here," he said.

"Oh, I can smell that," Liz said. "Like maple syrup and Elizabeth, New Jersey, all rolled into one." She raised us up, over her head. "I'll take care of this little spy for free." For a mad moment, we thought she might open her mouth wide and drop us in. Instead she marched out of the bedroom and into the kitchen, dangled us over the sink and dropped us down the drain.

☆   ☆   ☆

RAYMOND and Julia engaged in the act of physical love to completion only three times over the next year. Interruptions of various sorts kept intercourse to a minimum: the slow-burn realization from Raymond that he was engaging in sexual congress in the room in which his mother had slept for thirty years; Julia whispering the words "penis panic" into his ear as a joke, he pouts while she laughs; Julia suddenly becoming terrified of sperm and fetuses as they are reminiscent of parasitism in their own ways and so she flails and scratches and tries to sweep Raymond off the top of her as if sex were a judo match.

Julia became pregnant anyway and miscarried after two months. They mourned in separate rooms, Raymond and Julia, and together simply sniped and argued about anything they could that wasn't Peter Neads Fishman, *Plesiometa argyra*, the Sans Nom movement, or Z-Day.

One day, not long after the miscarriage, Davan appeared at the doorstep with a coffee cake and a pair of bookends. "Presents," he said.

"Come in," said Julia. The sun was low and in her eyes, so she squinted at him. She was wearing a house coat and slippers, looking older than Davan remembered her. Raymond wandered into the dining room from upstairs, hands in his pockets, and was ready to turn and go back up the steps, but Julia said, "Cake," so he stayed.

"You're going to be pardoned," Davan said.

Julia sipped her tea in response, leaving it to Raymond to say, "Oh?"

Davan waggled his hand. "We have someone in the White House. The pardon will be buried, a footnote of a footnote of an errata of a rider of an executive order counter-manding a bill that died in subcommittee, but it'll be there."

"What's the bill about?"

Davan rolled his eyes and tsked. "Federalizing library cards for children of illegal immigrants who are not them-selves illegal because they were born on the right side of a dotted line or something like that."

The three clinked their teacups together. "Bravo," said Raymond. Then he said, "How did you find us?"

"I've been here for a while. Since Z-Day, really. It's not bad for a town that doesn't exist."

"So, you just looked in the phone book that doesn't exist?" asked Julia.

"You're not in it, actually."

"We have cell phones only," said Raymond.

"I work for a publisher—nothing big, just catalogs. You're on the mailing list for some baby clothes thing."

"Yeah," said Julia. "I throw those out when they arrive."

The conversation wilted and soon enough Davan left. Raymond took the bookends, two pieces of Lucite shaped somewhat like the ziggurats of the Olmec-like tribe that once inhabited our place of origin, and started stacking the books in which he had chapters, or had reviewed for jour-nals, between them on the mantle place.

The next morning, Julia went up to the room that was only half-painted like a nursery, took her journal out from the slim drawer of the writing desk, found her favorite fountain pen, and got back to work on her short story:

June ~~wept~~ ~~sighed~~ ran her fingers through what was ~~once~~ left of her mousy brown hair. The cancer year had been a difficult one, and ~~Raymond~~ almond-eyed Astasio had grown ever more distant. He was now a memory of a line from a once-favored poem—"One like a wombat prowl'd obtuse and furry"—

On the margin she had scribbled: Astasio like poem or wombat? Fix later.

~~His~~ embraces, which were few and tentative, were now a strange sensation, nearly ~~chthonic~~ spectral. The last time she felt at home, alive, in his arms was at the New Year's Eve party, when ~~Liz~~ ~~Alysse~~ Leslie had walked in just after eleven 11:11? Fix later wearing the same cocktail dress and the same smile June always wore. The next morning, June was hung over from all the nerve-strangled champagne gulping, and three days later, after the feeling in her throat hadn't gone away, she knew something was wrong. With her marriage, with her ~~health~~ ~~soul~~ ~~life~~ ~~soul~~ life.

"Fuck it," she said, and she tore the page out of her book. She looked around for a wastebasket, but there was none. She cast her eyes around the room, even craning her neck as if that would allow her to see around the corner and out into the hallway where Raymond may have been lurking. Then she crumpled the paper up in her hands, ripped it into three smaller chunks, and ate them. Then she wrote on a fresh leaf of paper:

My name is Julia Ott Hernandez. I killed a man, started a massive protest movement, shut down the Internet, funded terrorists to the tune of tens of millions of bucks, received a Presidential pardon, learned to play the theremin, and lost a fetus, not *in that order but all due to the war between two nonhuman species—one insect, the other arachnid. I remain trapped in a world I didn't create but tried to change. I am a character in a story, clearly. Mad? Yes, in all senses of the word. If I must be a character in a story, I vow to make it my story!*

Then she stopped writing, and sucked on the nib of her fountain pen, leaving a bluish smear on her lip. She sighed and shut the journal, then opened it again and tore out the page on which she had just written. Crumpling it into a ball, Julia brought the paper to her mouth but did not eat it. Instead, she stood up, pushed the chair away from her with a flex of her hips, and marched down the hallway and steps into the dining room on the first floor.

Raymond was eating some soup he had prepared from a can at the dining room table. He was leaning over the bowl, his nose nearly touching the bumpy surface of the saucy red stuff, and shoveling in great tablespoons of potato and celery, He looked up, barely, when Julia entered the room. He said, "Hello." Julia threw the ball of paper at him; it bounced off his forehead and shot nearly straight up toward the ceiling, then landed atop his head and bounced off that as well, into his soup.

"Yahbye," Julia said. "I'm hitting the road, *viejo*. This was all a mistake. There are no epiphanies here for me in this dead world. I gave it another shot with you, and you shoot blanks. I don't care whether I live or die anymore, but I do care whether I live before dying." She nodded curtly. "Enjoy your soup. I know you had big plans for it."

She walked out of the dining room; Raymond got up and followed her, his hands wringing his mother's cloth napkin. "Where are you going to go? What am I going to do now?"

"I don't know yet," said Julia as she opened the screen door and stepped outside. "Watch the news!"

We are.

Nick Mamatas is the author of three novels, including *Move Under Ground* and *Under My Roof*, which have been translated into German, Italian, and Greek and nominated for the Bram Stoker and International Horror Guild awards and the Kurd Lasswitz Prize. Many of his sixty short stories were recently collected in *You Might Sleep...* As coeditor of *Clarkesworld*, the online magazine of the fantastic, he was nominated for a World Fantasy Award and for science fiction's Hugo Award, and with Ellen Datlow is he coeditor of the anthology *Haunted Legends*. Nick's reportage and essays on radical politics, digital society, pop culture, and everyday life have appeared in the *Village Voice*, *In These Times*, *Clamor*, *The New Humanist*, *The Smart Set*, and many other venues, including various Disinformation and Smart Pop Books anthologies. A native New Yorker, Nick now lives in the California Bay Area.

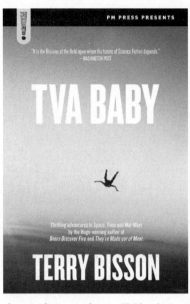

PM PRESS
SPECTACULAR FICTION

TVA Baby
Terry Bisson
978-1-60486-405-2
$14.95

Beginning with a harrowing, high-speed ride through the Upper South (a "TVA Baby" is a good ol' boy with a Yankee father and a 12-gauge) and ending in a desperate search through New Orleans graveyards for Darwin's doomsday machine ("Charlie's Angels"), Terry Bisson's newest collection of short stories covers all the territory between—from his droll faux-FAQ's done for Britain's *Science* magazine, to the most seductive of his *Playboy* fantasies ("Private Eye"), to an eerie dreamlike evocation of the 9/11 that might have been ("A Perfect Day"). On the way we meet up with Somali Pirates, a perfect-crime appliance (via Paypal) and a visitor from Atlantis who just wants a burger with fries, please.

Readers who like cigarettes, lost continents, cars, lingerie, or the Future will be delighted. For those who don't, there's always Reality TV.

"Bisson's work is a fresh, imaginative attempt to confront some of the problems of our time. It is the Bissons of the field upon whom the future if science fiction depends."
—*Washington Post Book World*

PM PRESS
SPECTACULAR FICTION

Fire on the Mountain
Terry Bisson
978-1-60486-087-0
$15.95

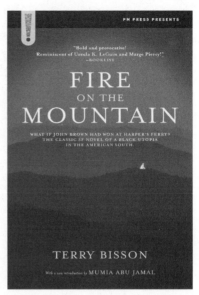

It's 1959 in socialist Virginia. The Deep South is an independent Black nation called Nova Africa. The second Mars expedition is about to touch down on the red planet. And a pregnant scientist is climbing the Blue Ridge in search of her great-great grandfather, a teenage slave who fought with John Brown and Harriet Tubman's guerrilla army.

Long unavailable in the U.S., published in France as *Nova Africa*, *Fire on the Mountain* is the story of what might have happened if John Brown's raid on Harper's Ferry had succeeded—and the Civil War had been started not by the slave owners but the abolitionists.

About the Author:
Terry Bisson, who was for many years a Kentuckian living in New York City, is now a New Yorker living in California. In addition to science fiction, he has written bios of Mumia Abu-Jamal and Nat Turner. He is also the host of a popular San Francisco reading series (SFinSF) and the Editor of PM's new Outspoken Authors pocketbook series.

"Few works have moved me as deeply, as thoroughly, as Terry Bisson's *Fire On The Mountain*... With this single poignant story, Bisson molds a world as sweet as banana cream pies, and as briny as hot tears."
—Mumia Abu-Jamal, death row prisoner and author of *Live From Death Row*, from the Introduction.

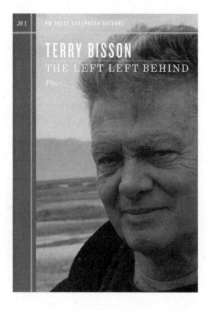

PM PRESS
OUTSPOKEN AUTHORS

The Left *Left Behind*
Terry Bisson
978-1-60486-086-3
$12

Hugo and Nebula award-winner Terry Bisson is best known for his short stories, which range from the southern sweetness of "Bears Discover Fire" to the alienated aliens of "They're Made out of Meat." He is also a 1960s' New Left vet with a history of activism and an intact (if battered) radical ideology.

The *Left Behind* novels (about the so-called "Rapture" in which all the born-agains ascend straight to heaven) are among the bestselling Christian books in the U.S., describing in lurid detail the adventures of those "left behind" to battle the Anti-Christ. Put Bisson and the Born-Agains together, and what do you get? *The* Left *Left Behind*-a sardonic, merciless, tasteless, take-no-prisoners satire of the entire apocalyptic enterprise that spares no one-predatory preachers, goth lingerie, Pacifica radio, Indian casinos, gangsta rap, and even "art cars" at Burning Man.

Plus: "Special Relativity," a one-act drama that answers the question: When Albert Einstein, Paul Robeson, J. Edgar Hoover are raised from the dead at an anti-Bush rally, which one wears the dress? As with all Outspoken Author books, there is a deep interview and autobiography: at length, in-depth, no-holds-barred and all-bets off: an extended tour though the mind and work, the history and politics of our Outspoken Author. Surprises are promised.

PM PRESS
OUTSPOKEN AUTHORS

Modem Times 2.0
Michael Moorcock
978-1-60486-308-6
$12

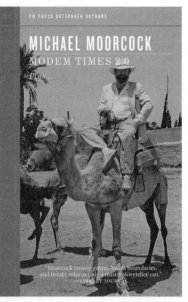

As the editor of London's revolutionary *New Worlds* magazine in the swinging sixties, Michael Moorcock has been credited with virtually inventing modern Science Fiction: publishing such figures as Norman Spinrad, Samuel R. Delany, Brian Aldiss and J.G. Ballard.

Moorcock's own literary accomplishments include his classic *Mother London*, a romp through urban history conducted by psychic outsiders; his comic *Pyat* quartet, in which a Jewish antisemite examines the roots of the Nazi Holocaust; *Behold The Man*, the tale of a time tourist who fills in for Christ on the cross; and of course the eternal hero Elric, swordswinger, hellbringer and bestseller.

And now Moorcock's most audacious creation, Jerry Cornelius—assassin, rock star, chronospy and maybe-Messiah--is back in *Modem Times 2.0*, a time twisting odyssey that connects 60s London with post-Obama America, with stops in Palm Springs and Guantanamo. *Modem Times 2.0* is Moorcock at his most outrageously readable--a masterful mix of erudition and subversion.

Plus: a non-fiction romp in the spirit of Swift and Orwell, Fields of Folly; and an Outspoken Interview with literature's authentic Lord of Misrule.

PM PRESS
OUTSPOKEN AUTHORS

The Wild Girls
Ursula K. Le Guin
978-1-60486-403-8
$12

Ursula K. Le Guin is the one modern science fiction author who truly needs no introduction. In the forty years since *The Left Hand of Darkness*, her works have changed not only the face but the tone and the agenda of SF, introducing themes of gender, race, socialism and anarchism, all the while thrilling readers with trips to strange (and strangely familiar) new worlds. She is our exemplar of what fantastic literature can and should be about.

Her Nebula winner *The Wild Girls*, newly revised and presented here in book form for the first time, tells of two captive "dirt children" in a society of sword and silk, whose determination to enter "that possible even when unattainable space in which there is room for justice" leads to a violent and loving end.

Plus: Le Guin's scandalous and scorching *Harper's* essay, "Staying Awake While We Read", (also collected here for the first time) which demolishes the pretensions of corporate publishing and the basic assumptions of capitalism as well. And of course our Outspoken Interview which promises to reveal the hidden dimensions of America's best-known SF author. And delivers.

"If you want excess and risk and intelligence, try Le Guin."
— *The San Francisco Chronicle*

PM PRESS
OUTSPOKEN AUTHORS

*Mammoths of the
Great Plains*
Eleanor Arnason
978-1-60486-075-7
$12

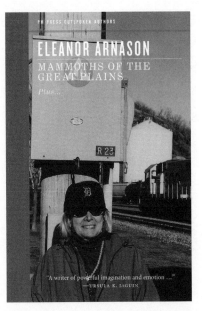

When President Thomas
Jefferson sent Lewis and
Clark to explore the West,
he told them to look especially for mammoths. Jef-
ferson had seen bones and
tusks of the great beasts in
Virginia, and he suspected—he hoped!—that they might still
roam the Great Plains. In Eleanor Arnason's imaginative alternate history, they do: shaggy herds thunder over the grasslands,
living symbols of the oncoming struggle between the Native
peoples and the European invaders. And in an unforgettable
saga that soars from the badlands of the Dakotas to the icy
wastes of Siberia, from the Russian Revolution to the AIM protests of the 1960s, Arnason tells of a modern woman's struggle
to use the weapons of DNA science to fulfill the ancient promises of her Lakota heritage.

PLUS: "Writing SF During World War III," and an Outspoken Interview that takes you straight into the heart and
mind of one of today's edgiest and most uncompromising
speculative authors.

About the Author:
Ever since her first story was published in the revolutionary
New Worlds in 1972, Eleanor Arnason has been acknowledged
as the heir to the feminist legacy of Russ and Le Guin. The first
winner of the prestigious Tiptree Award, she has been short
listed for both the Nebula and the Hugo.

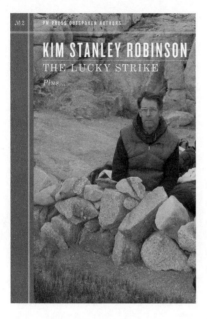

PM PRESS
OUTSPOKEN AUTHORS

The Lucky Strike
Kim Stanley Robinson
978-1-60486-085-6
$12

Combining dazzling specula-
tion with a profoundly humanist vision, Kim Stanley
Robinson is known as not
only the most literary but
also the most progressive
(read "radical") of today's top
rank SF authors. His bestselling "Mars Trilogy" tells
the epic story of the future colonization of the red planet, and
the revolution that inevitably follows. His latest novel, *Galileo's
Dream*, is a stunning combination of historical drama and far-
flung space opera, in which the ten dimensions of the universe
itself are rewoven to ensnare history's most notorious torturers.

The Lucky Strike, the classic and controversial story Robinson
has chosen for PM's new Outspoken Authors series, begins
on a lonely Pacific island, where a crew of untested men are
about to take off in an untried aircraft with a deadly pay-
load that will change our world forever. Until something goes
wonderfully wrong.

Plus: *A Sensitive Dependence on Initial Conditions*, in which
Robinson dramatically deconstructs "alternate history" to ex-
plore what might have been if things had gone differently over
Hiroshima that day.

As with all Outspoken Author books, there is a deep interview
and autobiography: at length, in-depth, no-holds-barred and
all-bets off: an extended tour though the mind and work, the
history and politics of our Outspoken Author.

PM PRESS
OUTSPOKEN AUTHORS

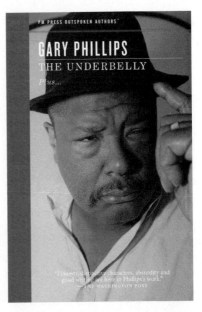

The Underbelly
Gary Phillips
978-1-60486-206-5
$14

The explosion of wealth and development in downtown L.A. is a thing of wonder. But regardless of how big and shiny our buildings get, we should not forget the ones this wealth and development has overlooked and pushed out. This is the context for Phillips' novella *The Underbelly*, as a semi-homeless Vietnam vet named Magrady searches for a wheelchair-bound friend gone missing from Skid Row—a friend who might be working a dangerous scheme against major players. Magrady's journey is a solo sortie where the flashback-prone protagonist must deal with the impact of gentrification; take-no-prisoners community organizers; an unflinching cop from his past in Vietnam; an elderly sexpot out for his bones; a lusted-after magical skull; chronic-lovin' knuckleheads; and the perils of chili cheese fries at midnight. Combining action, humor and a street level gritty POV, *The Underbelly* is illustrated with photos and drawings.

Plus: a rollicking interview wherein Phillips riffs on Ghetto Lit, politics, noir and the proletariat, the good negroes and bad kneegrows of pop culture, Redd Foxx and Lord Buckley, and wrestles with the future of books in the age of want.

"Magrady's adventures, with a distinctive noir feeling and appreciation for comic books, started as an online, serialized mystery. Drawings and an interview with Phillips enhance the package, offering a compelling perspective on race and class issues in South Central L.A."
—*Booklist*

PM PRESS
FOUND IN TRANSLATION

Lonely Hearts Killer
Tomoyuki Hoshino
Translated by Adrienne Carey
Hurley
978-1-60486-084-9
$15.95

What happens when a popular
and young emperor suddenly
dies, and the only person
available to succeed him is
his sister? How can people
in an island country survive
as climate change and martial law are eroding more and more
opportunities for local sustainability and mutual aid? And what
can be done to challenge the rise of a new authoritarian political leadership at a time when the general public is obsessed with
fears related to personal and national "security"? These and other
provocative questions provide the backdrop for this powerhouse
novel about young adults embroiled in what appear to be more
private matters – friendships, sex, a love suicide, and struggles to
cope with grief and work.

PM Press is proud to bring you this first English translation of
a full-length novel by the award-winning author Tomoyuki
Hoshino.

"Since his debut, Hoshino has used as the core of his writing a
unique sense of the unreality of things, allowing him to illumi-
nate otherwise hidden realities within Japanese society. And as
he continues to write from this tricky position, it goes without
saying that he produces work upon work of extraordinary beauty
and power."
—Yuko Tsushima, Award-winning Japanese novelist

PM PRESS &
GREEN ARCADE

A Moment of Doubt
Jim Nisbet
978-1-60486-307-9
$13.95

A Moment of Doubt is at turns hilarious, thrilling and obscene. Jim Nisbet's novella is ripped from the zeitgeist of the 80s, and set in a sex-drenched San Francisco, where the computer becomes the protagonist's co-conspirator and both writer and machine seem to threaten the written word itself.

The City as whore provides a backdrop oozing with drugs, poets and danger. Nisbet has written a mad-cap meditation on the angst of a writer caught in a world where the rent is due, new technology offers up illicit ways to produce the latest bestseller, and the detective and other characters of the imagination might just sidle up to the bar and buy you a drink in real life. The world of *A Moment of Doubt* is the world of phone sex, bars and bordellos, AIDS and the lure of hacking. Coming up against the rules of the game--the detective genre itself, has never been such a nasty and gender defying challenge.

Plus: An interview with Jim Nisbet, who is "Still too little read in the United States, it's a joy for us that Nisbet has been recognized here..." *Regards: Le Mouvement des Idées*

"Missing any book by Nisbet should be considered a crime in all 50 states and maybe against humanity."
—Bill Ott, *Booklist*

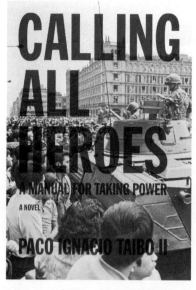

PM PRESS
FOUND IN TRANSLATION

Calling All Heroes:
A Manual for Taking Power
Paco Ignacio Taibo II
Translated by Gregory Nipper
978-1-60486-205-8
$12

The euphoric idealism of grassroots reform and the tragic reality of revolutionary failure are at the center of this speculative novel that opens with a real historical event. On October 2, 1968, 10 days before the Summer Olympics in Mexico, the Mexican government responds to a student demonstration in Tlatelolco by firing into the crowd, killing more than 200 students and civilians and wounding hundreds more. The massacre of Tlatelolco was erased from the official record as easily as authorities washing the blood from the streets, and no one was ever held accountable.

It is two years later and Nestor, a journalist and participant in the fateful events, lies recovering in the hospital from a knife wound. His fevered imagination leads him in the collection of facts and memories of the movement and its assassination in the company of figures from his childhood. Nestor calls on the heroes of his youth—Sherlock Holmes, Doc Holliday, Wyatt Earp and D'Artagnan among them—to join him in launching a new reform movement conceived by his intensely active imagination.

"The real enchantment of Mr. Taibo's storytelling lies in the wild and melancholy tangle of life he sees everywhere."
—*New York Times Book Review*

FRIENDS OF

These are indisputably momentous times – the financial system is melting down globally and the Empire is stumbling. Now more than ever there is a vital need for radical ideas.

In the three years since its founding – and on a mere shoestring – PM Press has risen to the formidable challenge of publishing and distributing knowledge and entertainment for the struggles ahead. With over 100 releases to date, we have published an impressive and stimulating array of literature, art, music, politics, and culture. Using every available medium, we've succeeded in connecting those hungry for ideas and information to those putting them into practice.

Friends of PM allows you to directly help impact, amplify, and revitalize the discourse and actions of radical writers, filmmakers, and artists. It provides us with a stable foundation from which we can build upon our early successes and provides a much-needed subsidy for the materials that can't necessarily pay their own way. You can help make that happen – and receive every new title automatically delivered to your door once a month – by joining as a Friend of PM Press. And, we'll throw in a free T-Shirt when you sign up.

Here are your options:

- $25 a month: Get all books and pamphlets plus 50% discount on all webstore purchases
- $25 a month: Get all CDs and DVDs plus 50% discount on all webstore purchases
- $40 a month: Get all PM Press releases plus 50% discount on all webstore purchases
- $100 a month: Superstar - Everything plus PM merchandise, free downloads, and 50% discount on all webstore purchases

For those who can't afford $25 or more a month, we're introducing **Sustainer Rates** at $15, $10 and $5. Sustainers get a free PM Press t-shirt and a 50% discount on all purchases from our website.

Your Visa or Mastercard will be billed once a month, until you tell us to stop. Or until our efforts succeed in bringing the revolution around. Or the financial meltdown of Capital makes plastic redundant. Whichever comes first.

PM Press was founded at the end of 2007 by a small collection of folks with decades of publishing, media, and organizing experience. PM Press co-conspirators have published and distributed hundreds of books, pamphlets, CDs, and DVDs. Members of PM have founded enduring book fairs, spearheaded victorious tenant organizing campaigns, and worked closely with bookstores, academic conferences, and even rock bands to deliver political and challenging ideas to all walks of life. We're old enough to know what we're doing and young enough to know what's at stake.

We seek to create radical and stimulating fiction and non-fiction books, pamphlets, t-shirts, visual and audio materials to entertain, educate, and inspire you. We aim to distribute these through every available channel with every available technology, whether that means you are seeing anarchist classics at our bookfair stalls; reading our latest vegan cookbook at the café; downloading geeky fiction e-books; or digging new music and timely videos from our website.

PM Press is always on the lookout for talented and skilled volunteers, artists, activists and writers to work with. If you have a great idea for a project or can contribute in some way, please get in touch.

PM Press
PO Box 23912
Oakland CA 94623
510-658-3906
www.pmpress.org